The Menu Match

MAPLE GARDENS MATCHMAKERS 3

PHILLIPA NEFRI CLARK

Cover by Wynter Designs

Editing by DP Plus

The Menu Match

Chapter One

"That's all I have for you today. If you liked my video, click the link below to subscribe and follow me on all of my other platforms!" Quinne kissed two fingers and waved them at her phone. Leaning forward, she tapped the screen to end the stream and sat back in her chair with a sigh.

People didn't realize how hard it was to keep up appearances. She always had to be on her best behavior, even when she wasn't in front of a screen. She was a celebrity in her own right, and it was exhausting.

She spun around in her chair and glanced at the clock on the wall. Her mother was expecting a visit today. A groan escaped from her lips and she eased out of her seat.

Alice Hart was the kind of woman who didn't take no for an answer. She was also up on all of the trends before they even became relevant. She was the one with connections. If it hadn't been for her, Quinne would probably still be working at a dead-end job.

Her mother was just... a little out of the loop these days.

Alice still thought she had an understanding of what people wanted to see. But there was a difference between being a little behind and being so out of touch that she actually suggested that Quinne make a video out at Maple Gardens.

There was no way. Quinne's followers had zero interest in a retirement community. She couldn't just put a dress on the place and call it something else.

But maybe she could make her mother believe she was still being helpful, still a big part of Quinne's success. She could record Alice with her little group of friends. Perhaps they'd all like to be interviewed. If nothing else, she could do a little puff piece and let one of the directors at Maple Gardens show it to the residents. They'd all get a kick out of that.

Quinne moved into the bathroom of her studio apartment and glanced in the mirror. Her silvery-blonde hair had the usual carefree look that took at least an hour to do every morning. The short style suited her and the lifestyle she led.

But her mother insisted that Quinne's style choices were the one thing holding her back from finding a husband.

Ha. What made her mother think she was interested in dating anyone right now anyway? She was too busy with traveling and events. There was barely enough time for her to enjoy a little time to herself.

Dragging a finger beneath one eye, she cleaned up a little makeup then slipped out of the bathroom and toward the door, only pausing long enough to grab her bag from the coffee table in her sitting area.

One short visit and she'd be free for another week. Okay, that wasn't really fair. She loved her mother and she didn't mind visiting her. There were just so many other obligations she had to deal with. Not to mention the group of friends she'd made at Maple Gardens weren't exactly the kind of people who understood her.

Quinne arrived at the main building at the retirement community and stared at the structure from her car. From the outside, no one would suspect that the majority of the people who lived here were well-off. When her mother had first shown her the flyer for this place, Quinne had been adamant that she didn't want to see Alice being locked away in some facility. But Alice wore her down. This place wasn't like the usual ones she saw on television or heard horror stories about.

Maple Gardens was a community of people who didn't want to live on their own anymore. Some of them had more needs than others, but her mother had thrived here and was happier than Quinne remembered ever seeing her.

She headed into the building toward the room where her mother was often found, but it was empty. In fact, it was practically dead in the complex except for exactly two residents. Not even the reception desk had anyone sitting there. An eerie feeling came over Quinne as she looked around the room.

Where was everyone?

Quinne picked up her pace as she strode along the corridor headed for her mother's little apartment. No Alice in sight. Something wasn't right.

This time, she jogged back to the main building, determined to find someone who worked at this place. If this was how Maple Gardens was being run, she didn't want her mother here any longer. They'd have to find somewhere with better supervision. How could a whole building of residents disappear?

The reception desk was still vacant.

The same two residents from earlier were eating lunch. At least that was something. Quinne hurried across the room to the couple, addressing the man, who had just finished a mouthful. "I'm sorry, but could you help me find someone who works here?"

The woman blinked as she stared up at Quinne. Her eyes darted from Quinne to the man beside her and she smiled. "Terrance doesn't speak much."

Irritation flooded Quinne's midsection. "Well, do *you* know where I can find someone who works here?"

The woman gazed at her blankly. Her brows creased and her lips pressed together. "There was something going on today. People were going out the door." Her eyes cut to Quinne. "I'm sorry, dear, my memory isn't what it used to be."

A groan escaped Quinne's lips. "All I need to know is if there is anyone here who can help me. I need to find my mother." Her tone held a little more bite than she intended and she reined it in. Had she gotten a mailer or any kind of notice that her mother wouldn't be here today, she might have been a little more patient. But right now, it was like the whole place had been raptured and the only two remaining people weren't going to be of much help. "Sorry about that. So, you don't know where they all are?'

There was no answer and she threw her hands into the air.

"They've gone to the pond to feed the ducks."

Quinne jumped and spun around. A man in a white

apron stood in the doorway of the kitchen. He wiped his hands on a towel, but he didn't smile.

"The pond?" She folded her arms. "What pond? My mother has been living here for at least a year. She hasn't said anything about a pond since arriving."

He jerked his chin toward the exit. "They just put it in about a month ago. Now we have ducks."

"You expect me to believe that the person in charge was willing to let everyone, including the staff, walk down to a pond to feed ducks?"

He shrugged. "I'm not in charge. I just make the food."

She snorted. "This is more than unacceptable. It's dangerous. These two clearly need supervision." She gestured vaguely at the couple who hadn't been helpful at all. "Where is the person who is supposed to do that?"

"You're looking at him."

Quinne's eyes narrowed, if only in an attempt to trick herself that she didn't need to blush with embarrassment. She shifted her weight from one foot to the other. "You're the cook. I doubt you have the credentials to—"

"I trained as a nurse before I decided to follow my passion and start working in the kitchen."

Her voice died in her throat and this time she did blush. The way he kept staring at her was unnerving, setting her on edge. She didn't like the feeling of someone having the upper hand.

Well, she was the one paying for her mother to stay here. She was funding his paycheck. Quinne frowned, swallowing the lump of discomfort the best she could. "When are they supposed to get back?"

"Quinne! You're early!"

She spun around to find her mother entering the common room ahead of the flood of residents that came with her. Cheeks flushed from whatever physical activity she'd just undertaken, Alice actually looked like she had enjoyed herself.

Of course she did.

Alice did things because she wanted to. Not because she was swayed.

Her mother flipped her long black hair over her shoulder and her blue eyes flashed brightly. The grays at the crown of her head were starting to peek through the dye job she insisted she keep up.

Alice reached up to touch Quinne's own locks but wasn't successful when Quinne ducked away. "Mom. You know I don't like it when you touch my hair. I have to be ready at a moment's notice for pictures and video."

Her mother smiled and shook her head. "You're always beautiful, dear. Not a hair out of place."

"Let's keep it that way."

Alice chuckled. "Okay." Her eyes shifted away and then back to Quinne. "I see you met the new cook. Chef Peter."

"Unfortunately, yeah." Quinne murmured. "He doesn't seem—"

"Isn't he handsome?"

Quinne rolled her eyes. "We've been through this. I'm not interested in dating anyone."

"I didn't say anything about dating him. I just asked if you thought he was handsome."

Quinne glanced over her shoulder, not surprised to find that the man had disappeared back into the kitchen. Quinne hadn't been interested enough to examine what he looked like. If pressed, she'd say he was average. Black hair and beard with silver streaks? Maybe brown eyes? It didn't matter. Chef Peter wasn't someone she cared to speak to ever again.

Quinne turned to her mother and her brows pulled together. "Why didn't you tell me you were going out on an excursion?"

Alice laughed. "I don't have to tell you where I'm going all the time."

"You should. I don't trust these people to keep you safe when you're out and about. Do you know how easy it would be for you to break something?"

Her mother scoffed. "Honestly, dear. I'm not *that* old. It was a quick walk down to the new pond. Oh, it was simply wonderful. I'm sure you could do some wonderful stuff for your job down there if you'd like."

There it was. More suggestions. "Thanks, Mom, but I've already got content lined up. I don't have—"

"Oh, I hope you don't mind, but I let Isaac Spencer know that you might be interested in having him pay you to do some content about this place."

"Isaac Spencer? Oh, the owner? I don't do content—wait, what? Mom! You know my brand has a specific standard. I do stuff for the younger crowd. No offense, but I don't have a lot of older subscribers. I doubt that they will want to see what it's like for their grandparents living at a place like this."

"No, I know that. I was simply making the suggestion that you might work with Peter in the kitchen. You do a lot of stuff with baking, too. I've seen those videos."

Quinne let out an exasperated sigh. "I haven't done baking videos for years."

"Well, I'm certain people would love to see that sort of thing again."

Quinne rolled her eyes. There was no convincing her mother she was wrong when she latched on to something like this. If Mr. Spencer contacted her, she'd have to respectfully decline. Maple Gardens wasn't the kind of place she wanted to promote. Not only that, but she wasn't sure how people would feel knowing she'd let her mother move into a retirement community when she could take care of her all on her own.

These days influencers could get cancelled for the smallest thing.

A couple of staff pushed out trolleys laden with plates and began serving lunch. Residents settled at tables, including Alice, who had a big smile as her plate approached. Quinne glanced at her phone.

"Oh dear," Alice said.

"What is it?"

Alice frowned. "Peter didn't give me a roll. I really love his little bread rolls."

Quinne rolled her eyes again. "Yeah, I know. I'm sure he'll come out again—"

"Would you please go get me one?"

Quinne stiffened and her eyes cut to the kitchen doorway. "Mom, I don't think I'm allowed—"

"Oh nonsense. I've gone in there before when he's forgotten something. You'll be just fine. I only need one little roll. And besides if we have to wait for him, my potatoes might be cold."

"Fine, but if he yells at me I'm going to blame you."

Alice smiled brightly at her. "That won't happen, I'm sure of it."

Shaking her head, Quinne strode toward the door. The kitchen looked like ones she'd seen in movies. Stainless-steel countertops, large stoves and ovens. Recessed lighting was mixed with pendant lights in different areas. The kitchen itself was actually impressive. She would have killed to have a place like this to do some of her baking videos.

Nope. She wasn't even going there. She wasn't a baker and those videos did nothing to get her where she was.

Besides, she owed it to the companies who took a chance on her to focus on their products.

A scream erupted from one side of the room and Quinne jumped. Her eyes swept through the kitchen until they landed on a little girl who was maybe nine or ten.

Quinne's eyes widened as the girl hopped off a stool and launched toward her.

"Quinne! It's really you! I knew you lived in Georgia, but I didn't know you lived *here*." The girl jumped up and down as another sharp squeal came from her lips. "I watch your videos every day."

A large metal door opened, revealing Peter. His eyes immediately locked on the girl and then shifted to Quinne. He heaved a sigh and shook his head. "Great," he muttered.

Chapter Two

It was hard to mistake Quinne Hart. The second Peter had seen her he knew Kat would freak out. He'd just hoped his daughter wouldn't catch sight of Quinne from the doorway.

He never expected the woman to enter his cave of solitude. Peter dropped a box of apples onto a nearby counter and raked a hand through his hair. "Kat. Leave the poor woman alone."

His daughter continued her excited jumping. "But it's *Quinne*. In real life!" She spun toward him. "You have to give me your phone. My friends aren't going to believe me."

Peter shot a look in Quinne's direction then brought his focus back to his daughter. "What do you need my phone for?"

"A picture. I must get a picture of her so they believe me when I tell them that she was here." Kat pivoted and hopped onto her toes once more. "Would you be okay with a picture? *Please*?"

"*Kat*," he warned again, but Quinne stopped him.

"I'd be happy to take a picture with you. It's no big deal." Her eyes landed on him and a tremor reverberated down his spine.

He'd seen her before, obviously. Despite him trying to keep his daughter off social media and away from the internet in general, Kat still knew all about the current trends and the people who were in the know.

Peter dug one hand into a pocket. The sooner he let his daughter get over her fangirling, the sooner this woman would leave his kitchen—and him—in peace. He held out the device and Kat snatched it with a huge smile.

Her bubbly voice filled the room, causing a smile to tug at his lips. It had been a rough year and Kat needed something to make it a little brighter.

Quinne ducked down to be on the same level as Kat in the pictures. Her arm was longer, so she held the phone up to take the selfie. With each additional picture taken, Peter couldn't help but be impressed by this woman's willingness to make a fan happy.

Kat took back the phone and swiped through the pictures, happy little squeaks coming from her lips. Peter got so caught up in her excitement, he didn't realize that he was being watched.

When he lifted his gaze to Quinne, he found her staring. His smile faded as he stared right back. "Is there something you needed?"

"A roll."

"A roll?"

Quinne nodded. "Yeah. A roll. You know, a small ball of flour and yeast that goes well when paired with a plate of lukewarm potatoes?"

He stiffened, the irritation returning. This was the

woman he'd expected when she'd materialized in the kitchen. "I'm sorry, there is only one per person."

"And my mother didn't get one."

Peter shook his head. "That's not possible. I put one on every plate myself."

"And you missed one."

He rolled his eyes as he dug through the box of apples to find the ones he'd be cutting to go with breakfast in the morning. "I don't miss."

Quinne placed her hands on her hips. "With all due respect, you missed her plate and my mom won't eat her potatoes without one. You might as well give me one so we can both go on our merry way."

One apple in hand, he faced her. "Like I said, I don't miss. Every plate was prepared the exact same way. I have a system and I know I didn't forget. Perhaps she ate it already and didn't realize it."

She gasped. "My mother is not senile."

"No one said she is. I'm only making a suggestion—"

Quinne marched over to a tray of rolls he'd pulled out of the oven just before she'd come into the kitchen. She snatched up a piece of bread before he had a chance to stop her, then she strode toward the door.

"You can't—"

"It's a piece of bread. I'm sure it would have gone in the garbage at some point. These people don't eat very much as it is." She slipped out of the kitchen, leaving him gaping at her.

Did that just happen? He shot a surprised look over to Kat, but she was still engrossed in the pictures of her with her role model. Pfft. Some role model Quinne was.

If Kat had been paying attention, she probably would have been just as surprised as he was.

Peter strode over to the door and locked it. The last thing he needed was more guests entering unannounced. Especially not tall, beautiful women with gorgeous eyes.

"See this one?"

"Uh huh." Peter mumbled. The numbers weren't where he wanted them to be. Maple Gardens wasn't ever going to be in financial straits, but he prided himself on being able to feed all the residents on the budget his boss had given him.

Hence the system.

"You're not *looking*." Kat's frustrated voice whined.

"I looked. I saw," he insisted.

"*No*. You've been looking at your binder this whole time."

Peter sighed. She was only ten and already she was acting more like a teenager than he would like. She was still supposed to be his little girl. He made an exaggerated show of looking at the phone she held up. Two happy faces smiled back at him.

His focus immediately shifted to the young woman —the woman who'd come into his kitchen and stolen a roll. Kat's smile rivaled Quinne's as she stood beside her. He couldn't remember the last time he'd seen his daughter that happy. "It's a great picture," he murmured.

"Great?" she scoffed. "It's the best. And I can't even put it online. Everyone at school thinks I lied."

"You're not getting a phone, Kat."

"I don't need a phone. I just want to set up an account—"

He lowered the clipboard in his hand to the counter. "Absolutely not."

"But why? All my friends have one—"

"You know very well why. You don't need to be part of any of that. It's dangerous out in the real world and even more so behind a computer screen, where you can't tell who is on the other side of things. No phone. No accounts."

She let out an exaggerated groan. "You're being so mean."

He turned back to the paperwork at hand. "I'm not supposed to be nice. I'm your father."

Kat let out another frustrated groan. "It's not fair."

"Life isn't supposed to be fair."

She muttered something under her breath and slid the phone toward him. "When are you going to let me get my own phone? I'm old enough. I know what's bad."

He shook his head. "No, you don't. You have *no idea* what's out there and I can't babysit you every minute."

She threw her head back and stomped over to the fridge. "I bet Quinne got to have accounts on social media when she was younger."

"I'd wager that sort of stuff didn't exist when she was your age."

"She's like twenty-five right now. I'm pretty sure Facebook was around back then."

Peter glanced at Kat. "She's twenty-five?"

"Yeah. Ten years younger than you. See? I bet you she got to have it." Kat yanked open the fridge, holding the door out while she stared at what sat on the shelves.

"Kat."

"What?"

"Shut the door."

"But I'm hungry and I didn't get lunch at school."

He pinched the bridge of his nose. "You're letting all the cold air out. I've taught you better than that. Figure out what you want before you open the door."

She glanced over her shoulder at him. "It doesn't have a window. How am I supposed to know what's inside?"

Peter got to his feet and marched across the linoleum tile toward her. He took the door and shut it before he faced her with folded arms. "You know what we have. And if you don't, then you ask. I don't want any of that stuff getting ruined because it didn't stay cold."

She rolled her eyes, the attitude returning.

His heart sank. How was he supposed to raise an almost-teenage girl all on his own? Between all the dangers that were lying in wait to do something horrendous to her—and everything that wasn't dangerous, but taught her to be disrespectful—he had his hands full. The arrangement with her mother wasn't working, not with Rachel traipsing all over Europe for extended periods.

Kat stomped toward the counter where she'd been sitting on the stool. She picked up his phone again and opened YouTube.

He could hear a female voice. Words like *julienne* and *dice* weren't the usual words he heard from that device when Kat was using it. On quiet feet, he wandered behind her and peered over her shoulder.

The woman was younger, but there was no mistaking her face. Quinne wore an apron, and she was explaining the different ways to cut food and why each technique was used.

"When you julienne something, you're going to cut it into long skinny pieces. This is going to help you cook food quicker and if you do it precisely it will give an elegant look to the dish. Usually you might do this when making stir fry..."

Quinne wasn't wearing a lot of makeup. In fact, pink streaks in her hair was the most unique thing about this younger version of her. Her eyes shone brighter, too. She looked like she was having the time of her life.

Kat stilled and looked over her shoulder at him. "What? You said I could watch her channel."

"Nothing. When was this posted? I didn't know she knew how to cook."

Kat returned her focus to the screen and nodded. "Yeah. She's got a lot of cooking videos. She was really good at it once, but she doesn't do them anymore."

"Why not?" Her technique put his to shame and suddenly he felt very self-conscious of her having visited his kitchen. That thought was clearly ridiculous. He was a professional chef, and she was a glorified celebrity.

His daughter offered him a half-hearted shrug. Together they watched the screen. When that clip was over the next one started. By the time he realized he'd been wasting his afternoon, they'd gone through at least half a dozen videos of Quinne. To his surprise, he now had new ideas for plating and quirky combinations which he was confident the residents would enjoy.

When he looked down at Kat, he found her smirking at him. "You like her."

He huffed. "Absolutely not."

"Yes, you do. You think she's pretty," Kat sang, "and you want to know more about her."

Peter patted her on the shoulder and shook his head. "At least you still have quite the imagination."

Her eyes widened. "You should invite her to do a show here."

He snorted, but the reaction backfired and he started to cough and his eyes to water. When he looked back at his daughter, he found her smile had widened further.

"Really, Dad. She should do a little show."

He didn't think it was possible, but her eyes widened even further.

"Then we could post it on a TikTok account and tag her in it and then everyone will know the photo was real."

"No."

"Then Insta if you'd only open an account, Dad!"

"Not Insta or TikTok or any social media."

He settled back into his chair and marked off a few things he'd missed when he'd started working through this paperwork. "Because I said no."

She let out a sound that resembled a large wild cat more than a ten-year-old girl and stamped toward the door. At least she wasn't directing her anger at him. Storming off he could handle. But being the target of her fury was a different story entirely.

Peter eyed the phone she'd left behind. His eyes bounced to the door then back to the phone before he picked it up. Leaning against a nearby wall, he swiped through Quinne's profile until he got to the earlier videos.

Maybe just one more wouldn't hurt.

Chapter Three

Quinne dragged her finger upward on her screen aimlessly. She needed new content, but she couldn't figure out *what*. There were no new games out that she was willing to showcase. No new content for the old games, either.

She hadn't been approached to do any other advertisements recently, so that left her to her own devices. She needed to come up with something that would make people flock to her channel again and boost her ratings.

A familiar video slid across the screen and she doubled back. Her thumb hovered over an older video of herself and she hesitated. She hadn't gone through the really old stuff for quite some time. She didn't even know if she was ready to watch herself fumble over the cooking terms and details that she gave her followers, back before she'd become famous.

Shutting her eyes briefly, she tapped on the screen and the sound came through the speaker.

"You all know I love cooking, but I'll let you in on a little

secret. I love baking so much more and I'll tell you why. Cooking is fun because you get to try something new. You pair a dish of something you already know you love with something so out of this world different that it becomes something new entirely. It's like learning how to decorate your house or pick out your new favorite outfit. But baking? I adore baking because it's like chemistry." Her laughter filled the quiet around her. "*I know what you're going to say. Science is* boring. *But it's not! When you bake bread or a cake or something else, you need to make sure the wet and dry ingredients aren't going to go to war in your pan. You're going to have to measure out the right weight or volume of something if you don't want your fluffy rolls to come out completely flat and lifeless.*" She held up a roll and turned it in her hand. "*See? This one...*"

The old Quinne knew what she loved and she didn't care a lick about what other people thought. She loved baking and that was enough to keep her happy. But things had changed. She'd matured. And she'd found out exactly how hard it was to be a creator who only did things for fun reasons.

She closed out of her phone and placed it on the comforter beside her. It would be nice if she could go back to a time when she could just upload content that brought her joy. But those days were long gone.

Sitting up straight in bed, a smile tugged at her lips.

Unless they weren't.

Although she had a default response with her mother of always saying she had content lined up, it wasn't quite true. Granted, there were offers all the time but lately Quinne found herself being pickier over her choices, no longer diving into something without it feeling...right.

Over the last couple of weeks, she hadn't been able to get a certain man out of her thoughts. There was something about Peter which intrigued her far more than the men her own age. He was direct, which was refreshing. And easy on the eye, if she was honest with herself.

Of course, what mattered was that he had the kitchen and the equipment. He even had a die-hard fan. Maybe she could get some backers and they could do a segment about cooking with the people who watched her channel. There had to be a company that would be interested. Maybe a manufacturer of kitchen supplies, or the owner of Maple Gardens, who hadn't been in touch despite her mother's suggestion. Heck, why couldn't she reach out to both? Everyone would win.

She climbed out of bed and yanked off her pajamas. It was already nine o'clock on a weekday.

Convincing the cooking supply company would be more difficult. While she was an influencer with a following, she hadn't released many videos showcasing her cooking skills. The more support she had the better this would all turn out.

A familiar sensation bubbled in her stomach, reminding her how much she loved this sort of thing. It had been a long time since she'd felt this surge of excitement. Quinne couldn't get dressed fast enough. She needed to visit her mother and see if she could arrange a meeting with that Isaac guy.

Once that was secured, she'd reach out to the baking companies. While she was interested in one of the bigger named brands, there was a local company here in Atlanta that might like to jump on as part of the team.

Oh, this was going to be so wonderful.

Quinne slowed her efforts as one thought crossed her mind. Peter would have to be on board as well. And it would be an even harder sell to get him to agree to his daughter participating. Most of her plans hinged on having a fan be part of the fun.

Maybe she should talk to him first. Then again, surely if Isaac was the owner slash manager he could simply tell his employees to cooperate.

Regardless, she needed to head over to Maple Gardens.

The whole drive over, Quinne's thoughts went into overdrive. She'd need to have a pitch ready. That wouldn't be too difficult, since she had old videos. This sort of thing was never done in an official capacity until there was a financial backer anyway.

Once she arrived, she strode though the front door and right past the reception desk.

"Quinne!"

Skidding to a stop, she spun around in search of the person who'd called her name. The young woman at the desk was standing, a smile lighting a pretty face. If Quinne remembered correctly, her name was Olivia. Quinne backed up a few paces. "Yes?"

"Your mom isn't here right now."

Her brows creased. "Where is she?"

"Some of the residents went on an outing to town."

This was just great. Waiting was not one of her strong suits. Sure, she could come back tomorrow, but she didn't even know if her enthusiasm would be the same. She could practically taste the success of this plan right now and that sort of feeling was contagious. "Do you know when she'll be back?"

Olivia shook her head. "I'm sorry. Sometimes they're gone for an hour, other times they're gone for two or three."

Quinne moved to the desk and leaned against it. "I really need to speak to her." Her eyes widened. "Or..." Quinne snapped her fingers. What was Isaac's mother's name? They were close. Shoot. She should have paid better attention to that information. "Margaret... Mandy..." She shook her head. "I can't remember my mom's friend. I actually wanted to speak to her. Is she here?"

"Do you mean Millie?"

"That's her! Yes. I'd like to see if she can arrange a meeting with her son."

Olivia tilted her head, a small smile on her lips.

"Oh wait! You're dating him, right? Engaged?" Quinne grimaced. "I'm terrible at this sort of thing. I'm so much better behind a camera."

"He's my fiancé." Olivia waved the fingers of her left hand and gave her an easy smile. "But I could probably help you. What do you need?"

Leaning her elbows on the reception desk, Quinne's expression brightened. "I don't know if you've seen any of my videos on social media. Normally I promote video games and the like to teenagers. But I had this amazing idea that I think could help out this place—and the residents."

Olivia's blank expression nearly caused Quinne's excitement to falter, but she pressed on.

"I used to do baking videos. You know, like replicating recipes from famous places. Or teaching people simple techniques. I thought it would be fun to do some of those videos here."

"Here?"

"Sure! I could have guests participate. Some of the residents might enjoy that. And it would give exposure to this place. I know that the residents sometimes get lonely."

Olivia nibbled on her lower lip. "So, what do you need Isaac for? Just permission? Are you wanting to use the kitchen? I'm sorry, I'm not sure exactly what you need."

"The kitchen, access to the supplies. And I was hoping he might be willing to get the chef on board with this."

"Peter? Oh, Peter wouldn't be interested in that sort of thing."

"No. I want to get his daughter to participate."

"You want to involve his daughter? That's a little... I don't know... weird, isn't it?"

"Kat and I met a few weeks ago. She's a fan. I thought for this series of videos it would be fun to include someone I usually do my videos for. I just don't know if her father would be up for it."

Olivia chuckled, lowering into her seat. She shook her head as she picked up her phone. "Yeah, I think you have a decent idea, but I really don't see Peter going for it. And I don't think Kat is even in the country."

"What do you mean she isn't in the country?"

"She lives with her mom in Europe somewhere. She only comes here for part of the year."

This was going to be a lot harder than she thought.

Olivia's eyes flitted to Quinne's. "I'll get you a meeting with Isaac, but I really don't see this working out if it hinges on having Kat involved. You might need to find another fan."

Her stomach tightened. She couldn't tell if it was because she realized she couldn't work with Kat, or if it had more to do with not getting closer to Kat's father. Interacting with Kat had been more fun than she'd expected. Olivia's recommendation of finding someone different just didn't sit well with her.

"Is Peter here?"

Olivia chuckled again. "Of course he's here. He's the cook. The residents eat three meals a day."

"Can I go talk to him?" Quinne gave a sharp shake of her head. "I should talk to Isaac, first, right? He'd be able to get Peter on board."

Olivia lifted a brow. "You're not serious, are you?"

"What?"

She sighed. "If I know anything, it's that guys don't like to be strong-armed into anything. And people in charge of kitchens like it even less. If I were you, I'd talk to Peter first. Feel him out. And if it doesn't work out, then you won't have to worry about talking to Isaac anyway."

Quinne shook her head. "No. I'm going to do this one way or the other. I can't explain it, but I know deep in my gut this is the path I'm supposed to take."

Olivia's look of disbelief was entirely expected. It wasn't the first time people had thought Quinne was crazy. They'd looked at her just like that when she started on her path to being an influencer.

She straightened. "I'll talk to Peter first, but please let me know when I can visit with Isaac. I know he's busy."

"Yeah. He's pretty busy right now. He's working on expanding Maple Gardens to other parts of the country. I barely see him these days." She peeked at Quinne.

"But I'll message him and let you know if he gets back to me after you're done talking with Peter."

"Thanks. I'll be right back."

The door to the kitchen was open, but Quinne couldn't bring herself to enter right away. She needed to get into the right headspace. She took a deep breath and then released it. This idea was a good one. He wouldn't be able to deny it. He'd see that it would be good for this place and even for Kat.

She straightened her shoulders and lifted her chin before striding into the kitchen.

"You can't keep doing this to us, Rachel." Peter raked his hand through his hair. "She's visiting a friend today." He let out a groan. "But she can't always be at a friend's house or doing homework in the kitchen here. You're meant to be part of her life." He paced back and forth as though he hadn't noticed Quinne's arrival. "What about school? She's getting settled, but doesn't know if you'll be taking her off again and when. That's no way for a kid to live. She needs stability." Peter turned, then jumped when his eyes landed on Quinne.

She offered him a strained smile and a small wave. His eyes darkened and he lowered his voice as he turned away from her. "If you keep this up, I'm taking you back to court and requesting a change of the custody arrangements. You can't just go on extended vacations whenever you want to. You're her *mother*." He hung up the phone and drew in a harsh breath before finally turning toward her.

"Hey," she murmured.

"What do you want?" he muttered. "I'm busy."

She stiffened. That wasn't the reaction she'd hoped for. He'd been politer when his daughter was present. It was entirely possible that she had overestimated this guy's flexibility.

When she didn't respond right away, he stopped what he was doing and faced her. "Well? Spit it out."

Quinne crossed her arms as if the gesture would protect her from his sour attitude. "I wanted to talk to you about something."

He heaved an exaggerated sigh. "I'd rather talk about the actual thing than discuss the action of talking about something."

"What?"

Peter twirled his hand around. "Five minutes. Then you're getting booted out of here."

Her heart skipped and she took a step forward. "I wanted to ask your permission to have Kat take part in a new series I'm planning."

Chapter Four

Peter stared at this crazy woman like she'd grown horns. He didn't know this woman except for the handful of videos he'd watched with Kat. There wasn't any reality in which he'd agree to something like that.

"No." He turned toward the fridge to pull out the ingredients he'd need for lunch.

"But—" Quinne's heeled boots clattered against the tile behind him.

Peter spun around, and nearly collided with her. "Are you being serious?" He glanced around the room with wide eyes. "Are there hidden cameras somewhere? I'm being punked, right?"

Her head reared back. "What? No! I am doing a new segment on my channel and your daughter gave me this idea. I thought she'd like to—"

"She's a *minor*. What don't you understand about that? What kind of father would I be if I let her do something stupid like this? Do you know how many terrible people have access to footage like that?"

Quinne opened her mouth but then shut it just as quickly.

"See? You know exactly what I'm talking about. I can't let her do it, because my one job as her father is to keep her safe."

"I can respect that. But you have to—"

"I don't have to do anything. Katherine is my daughter and I'm already dealing with a lot right now."

"Because your wife isn't..." One dark look from him and her voice died in her throat. She shifted under his gaze and tried again. "I mean, what if I watch her? Look after her."

Both of his brows shot up. "What?" He couldn't deny that her offer would solve some of his current problems. It seemed too good to be true and at the same time far too much to risk.

"I used to work at a day care center. And I know she's not *that* little, but until you find someone who can take care of her... She could hang out with me."

Peter didn't move. This woman had a background with children? Of course she did. Why else would she be interested in creating content for kids? It sort of made sense.

Quinne shifted, drawing his attention to her again as she mumbled, "If you don't want to accept my offer—"

He held up a finger. "You said you worked with children?"

She nodded.

"Do you have references?" At this point, if she could provide anything that would give him some kind of peace of mind, he'd be sold.

A small smile tugged at her lips. "Sure, I could get some."

"This doesn't mean I agree to Kat being on your show." He'd never change his stance on that. Children should never be put in positions where they could be taken advantage of. There was just too much evil in the world for him to be comfortable with it.

"My channel."

"Yeah," he muttered, "whatever." He took a few steps toward her. "And it's only *temporary*." Peter just needed enough time to figure out this whole custody issue and then maybe he could find a real nanny—someone who wouldn't put silly thoughts of social media in Kat's head.

"Sure, whatever you need."

Peter studied her for longer than necessary. Was he making a mistake? This could very well turn out badly. Then again, he wasn't getting that kind of vibe from her. It was possible that she had ulterior motives, but there were ways for him to combat that. He'd have a contract drawn up and everything would work out. "Okay. We can discuss your pay later. When are you available?"

"I can meet with you tonight."

He glanced at the calendar on the wall. It was a weeknight and the dinners would be all done by seven. Kat would be getting to bed around eight and then he could slip out. "Can you meet at eight-thirty?"

Quinne nodded again. "Of course. Where do you want to meet?"

"How about here? I can do some prep work for tomorrow while we go over terms."

The smile on her face sent a shiver down his spine.

It wasn't entirely a bad sensation, but it surprised him nevertheless. "Okay. See you then." He jutted his chin toward the door. "Now, if you will please leave. I need to get caught up on a few things."

He turned once more toward the fridge and when he glanced over his shoulder, she was gone. Peter let out a sigh. Kat was going to freak out when she heard about this.

"Seriously? Dad, I'm not a child," Kat muttered.

Peter whirled around to face his daughter. "You're ten. That's literally the age of a child."

"I'm almost eleven," she countered, "which is practically thirteen. I don't need a babysitter."

"Nanny," he corrected. Peter never should have told her that he was leaving in the first place. He knew better than to assume she wouldn't ask any questions. "Mrs. Johnson will be in from next door in a minute."

Kat groaned as she slumped against her headboard. "Do you really have to hire someone? I can handle myself. And when Mom gets back—"

The expression on his face must have been enough to catch her attention. She straightened as she stared hard at him. "What?"

He shook his head, turning as he shrugged. "I didn't say anything."

"No. But the way you were looking at me... I'm going back to Mom's home, right?"

Peter rubbed the back of his neck. "I'm not sure you are going back."

She stiffened. "But—"

A sigh left his chest and he faced her once more. "Your mother wanted to take a few months more... traveling."

"What does that mean?"

"It means you're staying a little longer with me." He didn't have to tell her the whole story, at least not until he met with his lawyer. For now, she could believe she was staying for a few extra weeks—a couple months tops—and that he was required by law to find supervision for her.

But that plan was dashed when he saw the look of utter confusion and disappointment on her face. "Come on, bug. We have fun together, right?"

She glanced at him, but the light didn't return to her features. "No offense, Dad, but I don't really think sitting in your kitchen is all that fun."

Her comment stung, but he couldn't blame her. All she ever did was sit on a stool with her sketch book. The first time he'd seen her take an interest in something was when Quinne wandered into his sanctuary and turned everything upside down.

He settled on the edge of her bed. "You might be mature for your age, but you're still my little girl. And the person I'm interviewing to keep an eye on you might actually be someone you like. You never know." Only he did know. If he did in fact hire Quinne Hart, Kat would be over the moon. That one decision might put him over the top in the favorite parent department—which would help his case when he finally confessed that he'd be fighting for full custody.

Peter offered her a small smile. "Can you trust me?"

Kat shrugged with a noncommittal grunt.

Already he was regretting a lot of the decisions he'd

made over the last twenty-four hours. Only time would tell if meeting with Quinne was going to be a good one. Peter leaned over and kissed her forehead. "I shouldn't be more than an hour or so. You have my number on the fridge and Mrs. Johnson—"

"Is coming over any second, I *know*, Dad."

"Right. Well, I'll be home soon. Goodnight, sweetie."

She rolled onto her side to face the wall. "Goodnight."

The temptation to tell her who exactly he was interviewing was strong. But once that information was out, there was no taking it back. Kat wouldn't let him pick anyone else, and he wasn't completely sold yet.

Peter got up from the edge of the bed and moved across the room. He stopped at the doorway and looked back at his daughter once more before shutting off the lights. With the door closed quietly behind him, he gathered his keys and made his way toward the door. Quinne better be ready for the interview of a lifetime, because Kat was the most important person in his world and he wasn't about to let just anyone enter her life without a thorough background check.

"A background check?"

"Yes. Is that a problem?" Peter looked up from the document in his hand. He couldn't deny the resume and references she'd brought with her on such short notice were impressive. Sure enough, she'd worked at several day care centers when she'd been in high school and college. He glanced up at her when she didn't answer his question.

Her eyes locked with his and that familiar chill coursed through his body. She shook her head and smiled brightly. "Of course not. Whatever you need."

Peter placed the documents on the kitchen counter that separated the two of them. "Why are you willing to jump through so many hoops for this? Don't you make enough money doing your computer thing?"

She ducked her head, a soft, breathy laugh slipping from her lips. "I make more than enough money. But the funny thing with being an influencer is that I have to keep creating content or those funds will run out."

He lifted a brow. "Isn't that a little stressful?"

Her eyes met his once again. "Is life really worth living without a little risk and danger?"

Peter stiffened. "Is that how you're going to treat this job? With all due respect, Ms. Hart, Katherine is everything to me. And if you're going to be as flippant with this—"

"No, of course not. Actually, I was going to tell you... I'm willing to volunteer my services."

He nearly choked. "*What?*"

"Volunteer," she repeated. "I don't need the money. But there was something else I wanted."

Peter pushed away from the counter, shaking his head vehemently. "I already told you. She can't be on your channel. My job is to keep her—"

"Safe. Believe me, I get it." She nibbled her lower lip, drawing his focus to it. "I don't know if you've seen any of my content, but I used to make videos about cooking."

"I'm aware."

Her cheeks colored. "You've watched my videos?" She shook her head. "Sorry. That doesn't matter. What matters is that I'd like to do that again. I want to go back to my roots. And the more I thought about it, the more I realized that cooking shows are making a comeback."

Peter returned to the counter, his skepticism keeping him in check. "So, what does that have to do with me... and watching Kat?"

She gestured around them. "This kitchen is perfect for that sort of thing. It's got all the supplies, the space—"

"No."

Quinne snapped her mouth shut and her eyes widened.

"This is my place of work. What makes you think you can just march in here and demand to use anything in this kitchen?"

"Well, I wouldn't be using the ingredients if that's—"

He shook his head again. "The answer's no. I can't have people in here who don't belong. Do you realize what that could do to my job? I'm not willing to get fired—"

"Isaac already signed off on it."

His stomach felt like it dropped to his knees. "You spoke to Mr. Spencer about this... without consulting me?"

She offered him a shy smile, one that only made him see her for what she truly was—an entitled woman who thought just because she had money and influence that she could get whatever she wanted. Quinne pulled out another sheet of paper from a nearby folder and pushed it across the counter. "I had a meeting with him after the meeting we had this morning. He said it sounded like a great opportunity to shed some light on the expansion of Maple Gardens. He's going to be putting more retirement communities all over the country."

The fury in his gut continued to grow like a bonfire out of control. His jaw was clenched tight and his words were spoken through gritted teeth. "You went behind my back."

Quinne's eyes widened and she shook her head. "No, I didn't. You don't own Maple Gardens. You're just the chef." She grimaced. "Sorry, I didn't mean it like that...but you're not the one in charge. I know better than to pitch this idea just to you. Without Isaac's approval, I wouldn't have even brought it up. I figured if I helped you out..."

He slammed his palm on the metal countertop. "Are you honestly suggesting some kind of quid pro quo?"

She flinched and he would have almost felt bad if it weren't for the fact that he felt completely cornered. His boss was on board. He needed a babysitter for his daughter, and Quinne was at the center of it all. How could he not feel like he was being manipulated into doing something he wasn't happy with?

"If it makes it easier, I planned on filming after you were gone."

Peter's gaze cut to hers. "What?"

"I won't get in your way. And I'll watch Kat for you so you can work without interruption. Isaac even loved the idea of me bringing a few of the residents in as guests on my videos."

He raked a hand down his face. This was really

happening. At this point, he couldn't back down—unless her background check came back with a problem. He highly doubted that would be the case.

So, what now? Was he truly stuck with an entitled, wealthy influencer for the next several months? In all likelihood that wasn't realistic. He knew women like this. They grew bored quickly. She'd probably only last a month or so and then she'd move on to the next fad. At least that would get him by until he could find a suitable replacement.

Peter sighed and reached for the documents on the table. "You can start in a few days." He gave her a sharp look when she grinned at him. "Probationary, of course."

"Of course."

"You'll follow every single rule."

She nodded.

"No social media, only two hours of television or screens, getting her to bed on time—"

"This isn't my first rodeo."

Peter shook his head. "I can't believe I'm actually agreeing to any of this," he muttered.

"You won't be sorry."

"I'm worried about *that*, too."

Chapter Five

Quinne bounced her toes on the floor and glanced at her watch. Not quite six. It was just getting lighter outside and it was still a bit too early for most of the residents at Maple Gardens to be up and about. Peter wanted her first day to be on common ground. She didn't know what she would do with a little girl at a retirement community, but she'd figure it out. She'd brought a tote full of things, but it had been so long since she'd spent time with children, she'd had a hard time coming up with what to include.

With her luck, the stuff she'd brought would be for children younger than Kat. Quinne would look like the idiot she was.

She didn't even know why she was so nervous. Did she have ulterior motives? Yes, but they weren't *that* bad. Kat would be a gold mine of information. Her die-hard-fan status made her the perfect person to get close to. Even if Quinne couldn't convince Peter to let her put Kat in her videos, she could still get ideas for other episodes that would draw more viewers.

Quinne glanced at the clock again, but the minute hand had only moved three notches. Olivia had told her to take a seat when she'd arrived, and the place was far too quiet. When was Peter going to show up? He'd said be here at six.

There was nothing more annoying than someone being late to a meeting they set the time for. Quinne nearly got to her feet to ask Olivia when the chef would arrive, but then Peter materialized from the kitchen.

She hadn't seen him arrive. Had he been here all along? Peter wore a black T-shirt, black pants, and a white apron. Nothing could force her to drag her attention from the way his shirt accentuated his toned body. Weren't chefs supposed to be on the rounder side?

Wait, why were these thoughts even crossing her mind? She was here on a mission. Starting next week, she'd be filming in the kitchen. She just needed to get the go-ahead from the companies who wanted to sponsor her.

That was better. She needed to keep her mind on the prize. No fantasizing over a certain chef who'd somehow become more attractive the longer she spent time with him.

A squeal erupted in the air. "No way! Dad! Why didn't you tell me you hired freaking Quinne Hart to be my nanny?" Kat raced across the room, passing her father and nearly colliding with Quinne. "You are, aren't you? That's why you're here?"

Quinne smiled warmly at Kat. "That's exactly why I'm here."

Kat squealed again. "Chelsey is going to be so jealous. I can't wait to tell her. O. M. G., this is going to be the best month ever."

Her eyes shifted to meet Peter's, only to find that he was watching his daughter. Was that a faint smile she saw? Peter hadn't seemed the smiling type. From the first moment she'd met him, Peter had been no-nonsense. He had one goal in mind and that was to protect his daughter. He had zero interest in a girl who spent her life behind a phone camera. She'd just keep reminding herself of that fact. Her job was more important than some silly crush that had suddenly accosted her without warning.

He finally met her gaze. "I'll be preparing breakfast for the next hour. You're welcome to find a conference room, spend time out on the property, or hang out in the kitchen. If you need anything—"

"*Dad*, we'll be fine," Kat insisted. She grabbed Quinne's hand and dragged her toward the open sitting area. "I have so many questions."

Quinne glanced at Peter over her shoulder. For a second she could have sworn the smile he wore was more devilish than angelic. And for the first time she wondered what exactly she'd gotten herself into.

Kat dragged her toward a couch and plopped down beside her. "Dad won't let me get a phone, but I watch all your shows at my friend's house and sometimes I get to watch them on my dad's computer."

She smiled at Kat's burst of energy. This girl was perfect. She'd be able to help with the shows Quinne had planned.

"My dad said you're going to do some cooking shows. Is that true?"

Quinne nodded. "That's right."

"What are you going to make? Are you going to do baking? Or cooking? Please tell me you're going to do some 'nailed-it' videos. I bet you'd be able to make the best stuff."

A laughter bubbled out of Quinne's chest. "Man, you *really* love my stuff, don't you?"

"It's the best!"

"Well, this new series I'm planning is going to be tough."

"It is?" Kat scrunched up her face into the most adorable look of confusion. "Why?"

"Because it's going to be a new series. Not only do I have to pull in my old viewers, I have to pull in new ones too. But the old ones don't usually watch this sort of thing. I'm going to need to know the best ways to do that."

Kat's eyes widened so large, Quinne thought they would pop right out of her head. "You want me to help you?"

"That's right. And if you want to ask any of your friends—"

"Tiffany. She won't believe this, but she's gonna want to help too."

Quinne laughed again. "Sounds good to me." They set to work writing down notes on different sorts of food that her audience might like. Then they brainstormed ways to include the residents from Maple Gardens in the clips, since Peter didn't want his daughter joining in—something that Kat was understandably disappointed about.

After about an hour, the residents started going into the dining room. Quinne nudged Kat. "You hungry? We could get something from the kitchen."

"Yeah, a little bit, but I don't like what my dad is making today."

"What's that?"

Kat made a face. "Biscuits and gravy. I hate sausage."

Quinne laughed. "I don't blame you. I hate sausage too."

Once again, Kat's eyes rounded. "Really? I've never met anyone who doesn't like sausage. It's like the thing everyone thinks is the best breakfast food in the world."

"Nope. I'm team crepes."

"What are crepes?"

Quinne let out an exaggerated gasp. "You don't know what crepes are?"

The ten-year-old shook her head. "It kinda sounds bad though."

Dang, this girl was adorable. "Crepes are like really thin pancakes, but kind of like tacos too."

"Now it *really* sounds gross." Kat grimaced. "Pancakes and tacos? Yuck."

Shaking her head, Quinne gathered her things in her arms and got to her feet. "Let me teach you. It's really very good. I'm sure your dad has some..." Oh wait. She'd promised Peter she wouldn't use any of the supplies in the kitchen. This could prove to be difficult.

"What?"

Quinne glanced down at Kat. "I don't know if your dad will let me cook in the kitchen. He probably wouldn't want me to use the ingredients either."

"It's gonna be fine. I use stuff in the kitchen all the time." Kat grabbed Quinne's hand and dragged her toward the kitchen door.

"Wait, are you sure? He didn't seem too thrilled about me doing any videos in the kitchen—"

"But you're not doing any videos today. You're

helping me get breakfast. That's what a nanny is supposed to do, right?"

"Well, yeah... but—"

"Then come teach me how to make..." She wrinkled her nose again. "Taco-pancakes."

Quinne was in the middle of laughing when Kat dragged her through the doorway into the kitchen. The laughter died in her throat when her eyes found Peter's. Those eyes of his had a way of making her feel small and insignificant, yet at the same time she couldn't help being drawn to him.

"Is there something you need?" Peter shut off the sink where he'd been washing a pan. He grabbed a towel and dried off his hands, before tossing it over his shoulder and facing her. "Do you need something to eat?"

Kat nodded. "Yep. Quinne said she could teach me how to make something."

Immediately, Peter's gaze locked with hers. "I'm sorry, sweetie, I told Quinne she can't use the kitchen for her show while I'm working."

His daughter dropped Quinne's hand and moved forward. "This isn't for her show. She said she doesn't like sausage either and she said I'd like tacos."

He lifted one brow and his lips tugged into a small smile. "Tacos aren't really a breakfast food."

"She means crepes." The words flew from Quinne's mouth in a rush. "But it's okay if we can't do it or if you don't have the ingredients. I can teach her another time. We can just have something else like oatmeal or fruit or—"

"Come on, Dad. I want to try it."

Peter put a hand on his hip. It was clear he was

battling with the idea and it was confirmed when he frowned at his daughter. "You don't ever try new foods, why this one?"

This time, Kat blushed crimson. "*Dad*, you're embarrassing me," she muttered. "Can she please just teach me? I promise I'll try it."

Peter glanced at Quinne once more and it took everything in her power not to drop her eyes from his. How was it that he could have this kind of effect on her? Standing there, trapped under his gaze, she felt like she was suffocating. Just when she thought she couldn't take it any longer, he let out a sigh.

"What ingredients do you need?"

"*Yes*!" Kat threw her fist into the air and spun around. "See? I told you he'd say yes. What do we need?"

"Flour, eggs, milk, butter, and a little salt." She said it in kind of a daze, finally able to drag her focus from Kat's father.

Kat hurried around the kitchen, grabbing a canister off the shelf, then to the fridge to get the milk.

Something bumped into her and Quinne let out a yelp. She spun around to find Peter standing at her side. "Just... don't make a mess, okay?"

"Of course not." Her voice caught in her throat as Peter brushed past her. He disappeared out of the kitchen and that was when she realized her heart was hammering like crazy. What was wrong with her? She wasn't usually this antsy around people and she refused to believe that Peter was the reason behind these sensations.

"Got it all. What's next?" Kat hopped up and down on the balls of her feet. "Do I need measuring cups? What are we putting in our tacos—I mean crepes?"

"Well, let's see. Does your dad have fruit or yogurt?"

"I think he has both. What kind of fruit?"

Quinne found a place to put her binder and the other supplies she'd brought with her, then followed Kat to the fridge. "I've used berries and bananas, but I bet we could chop up some apples really small if that's what you like."

"How about strawberries and bananas?" Kat pulled a small plastic container from the fridge and held it out to Quinne.

"Sounds perfect." Quinne put all the ingredients on a counter next to a stove. "Now all we need is a bowl and a pan."

Cooking with a child was a lot different than doing it alone, but it was probably the most fun Quinne had experienced in the kitchen for a long time. Kat was so inquisitive and her eagerness to learn rubbed off on Quinne in a way she hadn't felt in a long time.

It was hard not to enjoy herself. She showed Kat how to spread the batter around the pan thinly enough to make the best kinds of crepes. Then she taught Kat how to cut the strawberries and bananas using a paring knife. "You have to be really careful with those. They're incredibly sharp. So make sure to cut away from yourself and go nice and slow."

Every so often Quinne would find herself staring at Kat. She should have never stopped baking.

The hairs on the back of her neck stood on end and Quinne looked up to find the source of that strange sensation.

Peter stood in the doorway, watching the two of them cooking. For a split second she thought she'd caught him smiling. But she must have been wrong because he immediately turned away and got to work on something else. He avoided her gaze each time she stole glances at him.

She'd invaded his sanctuary. Of course he wouldn't be happy. On top of that, he was dealing with other problems, like his ex-wife. Quinne shouldn't expect him to be a happy-go-lucky kind of guy. As much as she wanted to help him, all she could do was take one thing off his plate and that was worrying about his daughter.

Chapter Six

Peter's chest was so tight he almost couldn't breathe. All day, from eating crepes in the kitchen to working on a project for school, he'd been pleasantly surprised by how well things were working. More than pleasantly surprised. The way Quinne was acting with Kat did things to him, things he couldn't control. Kat was a happy kid, despite everything she'd been through. She'd handled his divorce from her mother like a champ. Heck, she even handled her mother's extended absences with a grace that was beyond her years. But seeing her with Quinne proved she'd needed something more, something special. He hadn't seen her this lit up in forever.

On one hand he was thrilled. For the first time, he'd done something right. His daughter would love him forever because of this decision.

But on the other hand he felt incredible guilt. He wasn't the father he needed to be. He was always busy or working. And he didn't know how to raise a girl on his own. He was terrified of the teenage years.

The hardest part was watching just how natural Quinne could be with Kat. The way they worked together to make crepes was next level. Quinne was a natural. She was amazing. And he should never have doubted her abilities.

Their laughter filled the kitchen with joy.

For the rest of the day, he avoided looking directly at Quinne. Occasionally he caught himself thinking about her in some inappropriate ways. She was the nanny now and there had to be rules against him finding her attractive. And there were definitely rules against him dating someone right now—rules he had made up himself.

At one point Kat slipped out of the kitchen to get some pencils and paper because she wanted to draw. Quinne sat on a stool at the counter. She pored over the pages in front of her, a pencil between her lips. Some of her hair fell into her eyes and she tucked it behind her ear.

Kat would probably only be gone for another five minutes at most. He didn't know what spurred him to cross the floor toward Quinne, but suddenly he found himself leaning against the same counter as her.

She glanced up at him and smiled, before dipping her gaze to her paper. Peter cleared his throat, causing her to look up once more.

He rubbed the back of his neck. Finding the words to express what he wanted was harder than he thought. "I was wrong." Well, that was a start.

Her brows furrowed and she placed the pencil on the counter. "Okay?"

"I thought you were going to be a disaster." Dang it,

that was worse. The smile that tugged at her lips was more than surprising. She either thought he was joking, or thought he *was* a joke. Either way, he needed to backpedal and fast. "That is... I didn't think this whole nanny thing would pan out and I'm happy to say I'm glad I was wrong."

Quinne's smile widened. "I told you I was great with kids."

"Yeah. I guess I just didn't expect you to be that good."

She straightened in her seat. "Well, thanks. That's really sweet of you."

"Can I ask you something?"

"Sure." She rested her elbow on the table and placed her chin in her palm. "I'm an open book."

"How do you do it?"

This time she laughed. "What kind of question is that? You're going to have to elaborate."

"How can you connect with her so easily? It's like pulling teeth to get her to talk to me the way I've heard you guys chatting."

The smile faded from her lips, replaced by a thoughtful look. "Do we really seem connected?"

He nodded, praying she'd actually give him an answer that could help. If he was going to be taking over full custody responsibilities, he would need to know how to handle Kat the way Quinne was able to.

"I'm sorry. I don't know that I have an answer for you."

"Dang it."

"What?" The word escaped her throat in a small laugh.

He coughed, then cleared his throat again. "I

thought you might say that. I had just hoped that you would have some kind of easy answer."

Quinne reached for his hand. The gesture was likely meant to show him some compassion, but instead it elicited something electrifying within him. The spark that started in his hand ran along his nerves like a live wire all the way to his heart, shocking him much like he'd expect those paddles at the hospital would. He yanked his hand free, causing her to jump, but it didn't stop her from speaking. "Kat thinks I'm great because she only sees what I want her to. You're her father. Your relationship will always be different from those she finds interesting."

"With all due respect, that answer is even worse." He ran a hand through his hair and let out a sigh. "Lately I've been having a harder time connecting with her."

"Well, you'll be pleased to know that eventually, she *will* grow tired of me, and she'll move on to the next big thing. But you? You will always be her father. You're going to be the one she comes to when her life shatters after that first boyfriend breaks up with her. You're going to be the one she calls when she needs help with something that's broken in her new apartment. She's always going to need you."

He stared at her, dumbfounded. Of course, everything she had said made sense. But hearing it made all the difference.

"Besides, I don't think you'll ever have to worry about her not loving you. It's clear that she adores you more than anything in the world."

"She does?"

"Sure she does. You're all she wanted to talk about

today. She was telling me that she thinks you're the best cook in the whole world and one day she wants to learn to cook as well as you do."

His brows creased. "She hasn't shown an interest in cooking before."

Quinne shrugged her shoulders. "I'm just repeating a few of the things she said. Maybe you should offer to teach her how to make something. You could totally bond over that."

At that very moment, Kat wandered into the kitchen. She held a stack of printer paper and a fistful of markers and pencils. "I got it," she called. "Now we can really put a plan in place." She glanced from Peter to Quinne and back. "Do you need something, Dad?"

He shook his head. "Nope. Just seeing if you would like to go out for dinner tonight."

Kat's face broke into a smile. "We're going to eat out?" She whipped her head around to look at Quinne. "Wait, you're going to eat with us?"

Quinne's expression was one of deeper surprise. She stared at him with those wide eyes. He probably should have asked her if she wanted to go to dinner with them.

She turned to Kat and smiled. "Sure. I'll come to dinner with you guys. It will give us all a chance to catch up on what we did today."

Kat spun to face Peter again, throwing her arms around him tightly. Then she pulled back and with a serious gaze asked, "Can we take her home so she can see our house? I like it here and all, but I thought it might be nice to have her watch me at home sometimes."

Quinne was probably feeling trapped while they

spoke about her as if she wasn't right there. He chucked Kat under the chin. "You know what? I think tonight we'll just stick with dinner. We can discuss having Quinne visit another time."

He had expected her to pout over that answer. But instead, she shrugged. "Okay." Kat climbed onto the stool and beamed at Quinne. "You're gonna love it. Dad lives in a small house, but we have a lot of land. There's a garden and a trampoline. Oh, and the kitchen is bigger than this one. It takes up like half of the whole house..."

Peter forced himself to stop staring. It was crazy how easy it had become to let this woman into his life. Part of him wanted to fight what was happening—this path he had decided to take. But deep down he knew he couldn't.

Or maybe he actually *didn't* want to.

He couldn't tell if Quinne was grateful for his intervention with Kat. There was a possibility of that. But on the other hand, she might not even care. Her gaze locked with his. Warmth swirled in his chest, filling his whole body with something strange. The only way to describe what he was feeling was that time had slowed down. She had him pinned with those blue eyes of hers. The smile that played at her lips only made that feeling intensify.

Kat tugged on his arm, breaking the spell. "Come on, Dad. I'm hungry."

"Right. Let's get going then, shall we?"

His daughter pulled him toward the door and it took every ounce of self-control he had not to look over his shoulder to make sure Quinne was following them. Once they were outside, she headed for her car and Kat yanked at him to get him to stop. "Wait. I thought we were going to drive."

Peter glanced up at Quinne who gave them a little wave. "I'll just follow you there. That way you don't have to bring me back here."

He turned to Kat and pulled her forward. "See? This is better. She'll be there."

"But I wanted to sit with her. Can I ride with her instead?"

Peter chuckled. "You barely know her. You're not going to ride in the car of a stranger."

She pouted. "Quinne isn't a stranger. She's awesome and she's my friend."

"Well, until she becomes *my* friend, you're not going anywhere in her car."

Kat groaned. "*Dad*, you're being so uncool."

He looped his arm around her neck and pulled her close to kiss the crown of her head. "I'm not supposed to be cool. I'm supposed to keep you safe." She rolled her eyes and he chuckled. "Did you have fun today?"

"Obviously."

"What was your favorite part?"

Immediately, her face brightened and she spun around to face him. Kat's features grew animated and her hands flew as she spoke. "Quinne asked me to come up with some ideas to get her viewers up. She said she wanted to make sure..."

The words that flew from Kat's mouth were hard to follow. He couldn't tell if it was because he wasn't up on social media, or if it was just the age barrier between himself and his daughter. Things were so different than when he was a kid. It was wild the way kids today knew their way around devices and the internet, and that fact terrified him.

Quinne was the epitome of what he was worried about. In no time, Kat could turn into a young woman who could very well maneuver the web without his knowledge. He was entirely aware of the possibilities but, more than that, he knew that there was nothing he could do to stop it.

He found solace in the one place he hadn't expected.

The one person who represented everything he hated about social media was also the person who was proving people like her weren't so bad. At first Quinne had appeared to be the worst kind of entitled. But she continued to surprise him. She wasn't as entitled as he'd thought. There was a human behind all of the bravado, someone he might actually want to get to know a little better.

"Dad?"

He jumped and glanced down at Kat where she stood holding the car door open. Her head was tilted and a look of confusion and slight amusement filled her face.

"What's so funny?"

"What? Nothing. Why do you ask?"

"You're smiling."

Chapter Seven

Quinne sat across from the father–daughter duo, but couldn't bring herself to look up. She could feel Peter's eyes on her and for the life of her she couldn't figure out what she'd done wrong.

That had to be the only reason he was staring at her. She'd done something to upset him. Had Kat told him something in the car that made him second-guess his decision to hire her?

She racked her brain, going over everything they'd done during the day. Quinne couldn't think of anything that was inherently bad. It had been a lot of fun to hang out with Kat and figure out what made her viewers tick. It had given her a refreshing outlook on her career. No longer did she feel like she was drowning in her decisions.

Squirming in her seat, she flipped the menu over and her vision blurred. She couldn't stop thinking about what Peter might be thinking—which was ridiculous. She didn't need to worry about him. If he wanted to fire her, he would have done so before treating her to dinner, right?

Against her better judgment, she glanced up.

Peter wasn't looking at her. Had she totally lost her mind?

Probably. Those serious looks he'd been giving her back at Maple Gardens must have really messed with her head. He didn't have any interest in her. But her obsession with thinking he did said a lot more about her than anything else.

Was Peter attractive? Sure.

Did that mean she wanted to get caught up in something serious with him?

Of course not.

There. She'd figured everything out. She was fine. This was just a job and she was getting a lot more out of it than she'd expected. Her gaze shifted to Kat and the girl looked up at that exact moment. Quinne leaned over the table. "What do you like to get here?"

Kat shrugged. "I usually just eat French fries."

"*Just* French fries? I'm sure there's something here that you like besides that."

Peter chuckled, drawing Quinne's attention. He shook his head. "Kat doesn't eat much. There are like six things she *will* eat."

Kat scoffed. "I eat more than six things."

Quinne's eyes bounced from Peter to Kat and back, disbelief the only emotion she could pin down. "You're kidding."

"I eat more than six things," Kat groaned.

"Wait, so you don't eat all the stuff your dad makes?"

Kat wrinkled her nose and Peter chuckled. "You

might as well tell her, sweetheart. She's trying to do a cooking show."

"She's doing a *baking* show, dad. That's different. I like that kind of stuff."

"Ah," Peter laughed again. "So you're excited about the baked goods, but if she were making meals, you wouldn't be?"

Quinne couldn't believe what she was hearing. "Wait, so what about this morning? You tried the crepes."

Peter made a face. "That's what I was trying to say. She's not the most adventurous eater. I was impressed she ate it at all. But to be fair, Kat *does* like pancakes. Oh, and fruit. Maybe that's why she was willing to try it." He leaned forward almost conspiratorially, much to Kat's displeasure. "Then again, maybe she didn't want to be embarrassed in front of you."

"*Dad*! Geez!"

Peter laughed again. "Does this mean you'll try something new tonight? Are you going to prove me wrong?"

Kat's eyes darted to Quinne then dropped to the menu in front of her. "I just want fries and a shake."

"Suit yourself." Peter turned back to his menu and Quinne couldn't help but watch how deflated Kat looked.

"Hey. It's okay. You know what? When I was younger, I went through a phase where I wouldn't eat any fruit or vegetables at all. None of it. Well, I'd eat potatoes, but that's not really a vegetable, is it?"

Kat peeked at her but didn't say anything.

"Anyway, as I got older, I realized I was missing out on a lot of stuff by not trying any of it. So one day I told myself I'd try just one thing. That was all I was willing to do. Just a bite. And every day since then, I try to do the same thing. One new thing."

Kat still wasn't speaking, but out of the corner of Quinne's eye, she could tell that she'd caught Peter's attention.

"Am I going to like everything I try? Nope. Do I have to like most of it? Nu-uh. But it's kind of fun doing it. Like riding a rollercoaster. You have to try it before you know if you'll like it, right?"

A small smile replaced the dejected look on Kat's face. "I guess so."

"You don't have to try anything today. You already tried the crepes, right?"

Kat nodded.

"Well, we can come up with something new tomorrow if you'd like."

"Okay." Kat straightened in her seat and her confidence returned. "I really do like baked stuff, though. Like cakes and cookies. I like bread, too."

"Good. Because I think one of the first recipes I need to dig up is my sourdough bread."

Kat wrinkled her nose. "What is *that*?"

"Most restaurants sell sourdough bread. You've probably tried it without realizing it. But the cool thing about that kind of bread is that it's like a science experiment. You only need three ingredients. Flour, water, and starter." She leaned closer to Kat again, her voice lowering. "Guess what the starter is made out of."

Kat stared at her with wide eyes as if Quinne were telling a suspenseful story around the campfire. "What?"

"Flour and water."

"That doesn't make any sense."

Quinne shrugged. "I know. But that's how it's made. It's really fun to make, but you have to be careful because it's got an attitude."

Kat laughed. "So it's like a teenager of bread."

Quinne laughed too. "I like that! Sourdough is the teenager of bread. We could use that on my video. Would that be okay?"

"Sure." Kat beamed, then turned her smile to her father. "See? I have good ideas, too."

"Sounds like it," Peter murmured. His focus flitted to Quinne and that stare of his had her heart thundering all over the place. It wasn't fair that he could elicit those reactions in her body. She was acting just like a teenager with a crush.

Quinne tore her gaze away from him just as their waitress arrived. She took their order for drinks then hurried away, taking the reprieve with her.

"Well, what is everyone getting?" Peter asked. "I guess we already know what Kat wants. So, Quinne, what would you like?"

"Do you have any suggestions?" She always hated ordering food on dates. She could never tell what the other party was willing to pay. Of course, she could afford to pay for her own meal, but most of the time, the guy wanted to be a 'gentleman' and she was left hungry more often than not.

Peter folded his menu up. "Well, I can't really make a suggestion unless I know if you have any dietary restrictions."

"Dietary restrictions? Like allergies?"

He shook his head. "People like you... aren't you all

vegan or vegetarian or like gluten free or watching your weight?"

"Me? Of course not. In fact, I could probably eat more than you in one sitting."

His brow lifted before his eyes swept over her frame. "I *doubt* that."

"Wanna bet?"

Peter stiffened. "What?"

"Come on, you're not scared, are you?"

Kat laughed and nudged her father. "You should do it."

"What am I doing exactly?"

"Are we doing an eating competition, or are we just making a bet? Because I can do either." Quinne winked at Kat, loving the way she'd finally been able to get Peter off balance after feeling that exact way all day.

"Sure. Let's do a competition. Whatever I eat, you have to eat. Every single bite. And if you can't—"

"Oh, I'll be able to. But what about you? If I eat everything you do, then I get to pick the dessert and you have to eat what I do."

"Deal."

Their waitress returned and Peter leaned forward, his voice lowering just enough to send chills down her spine. "Don't mess with a chef."

She matched his position and tone of voice. "Don't mess with someone who has entered her share of eating competitions."

The look of shock on his face was worth revealing her surprise now rather than when she won. He was in for it and he had no idea.

"Wait, what?"

Quinne grinned.

Peter's chin lifted. "We'll have the bottomless pasta and breadsticks."

Pasta was perfect. "I will eat you under the table and then you can eat your words."

This time Kat laughed. "This is awesome. Dad, I need your phone."

He was in the middle of looking like he had some big retort, but he stopped and stared at his daughter. "What? Why do you need my phone?"

"Oh, I'm not missing out on recording this." She turned toward Quinne. "It's okay, right? I can record this and you will post some of it to your channel?"

She shrugged. "Sure, why not?" Her eyes landed on Peter once more and his stern expression was enough to spur her to continue. "As long as your dad is okay with it."

Peter's jaw tightened as he battled with something internally.

"So, two bottomless pasta dishes?"

They all jumped and looked back to their waitress. Had everyone forgotten the poor woman was still taking their order? Quinne flushed and retrieved all the menus. "Just need Kat's order. What do you want?"

Kat sat back in her seat, her eyes bouncing from Quinne to her father and back.

"Didn't I already say? She's going to get fries. That's what she always does." Peter's voice held a teasing note, but Quinne could hear the barest amount of concern beneath the surface.

Quinne leaned toward Kat. "How about this. You order your fries and I'm going to get us all an appetizer —something new."

Kat's eyes widened with what could only be described as fear and Quinne had to hold back a laugh.

"One bite. That's all. You do that, and you can beat your dad, too."

Once more, Kat looked at her father. Then an expression of pure stubbornness crossed her features. "Okay. I'll do it."

Quinne turned to the waitress with an apologetic smile. The woman had already earned her tip for the evening. "We'll have the lettuce wraps with the sesame chicken." She avoided looking at Kat. Drawing attention to her anxiety would only make this harder.

While it was simple enough to avoid looking at the girl, she couldn't stop herself from meeting Peter's gaze. It felt like something was shifting between them. She couldn't put her finger on it, though. It was as if he were willing to be more open with her.

Granted, that could all be in her imagination. Or the feeling could be associated with the fact that Kat was with them. Either way, when she locked her gaze with his, that familiar chill swept through her.

His eyes held hers, freezing her, mesmerizing her, and making it impossible to do anything. Then his mouth twitched and his lips formed the silent words, 'thank you'.

Warmth flushed right through her, replacing the strange chills and making her feel validated in some way. She tore her eyes from his and fingered the napkin in her lap, rubbing the canvas fabric between her finger and thumb.

It shouldn't mean that much to her—his appreciation. She wasn't doing it for him. None of this was for him. A knot formed in her stomach with the realization.

This whole thing had started because she wanted something, and she'd figured out a way to get it. That was what she always did.

She set her eyes on the prize and nothing could stand in her way.

Except...now things felt a little different. Suddenly, she didn't care *as much* what she was getting out of this.

Yes, something had definitely shifted.

Chapter Eight

Peter had to be seeing things. There was no way Quinne had the space in her stomach for the amount of food she was putting away. "Do you have a hollow leg or something?"

She stopped, her fork mid-air. For a moment he thought he might have offended her with his statement, but then she took her bite, chewed, swallowed, and laughed. "Do you know, my dad used to say that exact thing when I was a kid. I was always hungry and he said he didn't know how I could constantly be eating."

"Well, we have that in common." His stomach gurgled, angry with him for eating so many carbs. He should have paced himself better. He'd only completed two servings of his fettuccini and Quinne was nearly halfway done with her third plate.

He looked down at his own dish with despair. She was right. He didn't stand a chance. She was running circles around him, and he was pretty sure she'd eaten at least two extra breadsticks.

Peter caught his daughter's gaze. Kat had been completely enthralled by this whole competition. But before any of it happened, she did what she'd promised. She'd taken a bite of the sesame chicken.

Yes, she made a face. But she did swallow her mouthful without complaint.

Quinne was a surprise in more ways than one. He didn't get it. None of this made any sense. He was usually such a good judge of character.

Those thoughts immediately made him feel ten times guiltier. No one acted the same in public as they did behind closed doors. Quinne was no exception. He had been willing to judge her based on her social media posts instead of getting to know her face to face.

How could he have been so judgmental?

What kind of example was he setting for his daughter?

Quinne wagged her fork at him. "Are you giving up? Or do we need to get you another plate?"

He glanced at her, then at the plate, and his stomach growled at him once more. With a resigned sigh, he placed his fork on the plate and sat back in the booth. "Get me the white flag and I'll wave it. You beat me."

Kat let out an excited sound he had never heard before, causing him to glance at her sharply. She ducked her head and a small laugh bubbled from her lips.

"If I didn't know any better, I would assume you were betting against me."

She blushed and laughed again. "I mean, Dad... it's *Quinne Hart*. She's pretty amazing."

His focus swiveled to Quinne. "Yeah, I suppose you're right."

Quinne's expression sobered.

Had he just said that out loud? Shoot. The last thing he needed was to mess up everything he had going for him right now—and that meant Quinne and her budding relationship with Kat. He couldn't afford to find another nanny. Due to his ex being MIA, he didn't have the luxury of making any other plans.

Peter cleared his throat and glanced away. There was nothing he could say to fix this. He knew better than to bury himself deeper in a problem and that was exactly what he'd do if he opened his mouth to say a single word.

The waitress materialized out of nowhere and he muttered, "Thank goodness."

"Will anyone be wanting desserts this evening?"

"Absolutely not."

"Oh, I think we're good."

"I want ice cream."

All three of them spoke at the same time, causing a smile to spread across the waitress's face. "I can give you three another moment if you'd like..."

Peter gave Kat a pointed look. "You ate fries tonight. Do you really think you should get ice cream?"

"I ate some chicken too," she argued.

Quinne laughed, drawing his attention. Normally he wouldn't have taken notice of something so simple. But for some reason his body had gone rogue. His ears perked up any time she made a sound. His eyes found hers whenever he had an excuse that didn't make him look like a crazy stalker.

What was happening to him?

Had he gone completely off the deep end?

Quinne tilted her head toward Kat. "She has a point, you know. She *did* eat that teeny-tiny bit of chicken that a little bug could have eaten. But if anyone deserves ice cream it's me."

Kat gasped and her mouth fell open. "I ate more than that. You saw. Both of you did. I should get ice cream because I tried something new."

He was just about to cave when Quinne pushed the appetizer plate toward Kat. "You know what would really convince him?"

Kat made a face.

Quinne shrugged and held out her hand to study her fingernails. "Suit yourself. But let me point out that the best way to get what you want is to offer something someone else can't refuse." She winked at Kat then her gaze bounced to meet his.

That was exactly what she'd done to him. She'd made him an offer he couldn't refuse.

No wonder he felt both grateful and trapped at the same time.

Kat picked up her fork with a sigh.

Peter fought the instinct to let his mouth fall open and stare at Quinne like he'd been trying to avoid all evening.

The woman was a genius.

No one had been able to get Kat to do this sort of thing.

Maybe Quinne was secretly a sorcerer.

Kat stabbed another piece of chicken, turned her fork around to study it, and then pushed it into her mouth.

This time she didn't even make a face. She chewed

and swallowed then, without missing a beat, turned toward him. "There. *Now* can I have ice cream?"

"I don't see why not."

Kat beamed. "I want the chocolate sundae with sprinkles and whipped cream. *Lots* of whipped cream."

"Alright, kiddo. Easy. Maybe we should just pick something up on the way home."

She frowned. "But this place has the best ice cream. Remember when I got it last time?"

He glanced at Quinne. "I don't have any memory of that, sweetie."

"I was like five."

Peter chuckled. "Well, that would explain it. I didn't realize you would remember something from so long ago."

She nodded. "It's the best." She turned toward Quinne. "They even put on a cherry."

"Oh, well if they have a cherry..." Quinne met his gaze and held it for one more breath-stealing moment.

"Fine. You can get your ice cream here, but that's it."

Kat squealed as she hopped up from the table. "Please tell the lady what I want. I'm going to the restroom." She hurried off before Peter could tell her to wait. The words died in his throat as he realized he now sat alone with a woman he couldn't seem to find his place with.

She was his daughter's nanny. But she was so much more than that. She would be working with him—sort of—at Maple Gardens. He wasn't an idiot. The videos she had brainstormed with Kat would help bring positive attention to the retirement community.

Beyond those connections, she was also managing

to be a good influence on his daughter. He'd have to be blind not to see that. As much as he hated the reality, he had to admit that Quinne knew how to talk to his daughter. She could relate to Kat in a way he could only dream.

On top of that, he was fully aware that his relationship with his daughter was doomed to only get worse. She'd be a teenager sooner than he'd like to accept. One day she would do everything in her power to avoid him. The days of his sweet little girl looking up to him were all but gone.

Quinne was the first to break eye contact. She picked up her fork, but instead of eating she swirled the remainder of her food around on her plate. "Thank you for this—tonight."

He huffed. "I think I should be the one thanking you." Peter shifted in his seat and leaned over his place setting. "Kat has never tried something like what she tried tonight. I don't know how you do it."

She smiled and lifted a shoulder, but didn't meet his gaze. "It's probably just because of my videos. It's nothing."

"It's *not* nothing. The way you so effortlessly nudged her in the right direction without sounding judgmental or overbearing—I just can't—"

"I'm not her father." Quinne's voice was quiet. She squirmed in her seat and shook her head. "I'm not a parent. Kids have a hard time taking advice or guidance from their parents, which is ironic considering that's where they should get most of their learning from."

"Yeah," he murmured, "ironic."

"I'm just someone she looks up to for the moment. One day she will wake up and she won't like me so much. Or she'll move on to a pop star or a favorite actor." A small smile touched her lips. "One day I will be irrelevant and my fans will forget all about me."

He didn't know how to respond. This conversation had taken an unexpected turn. She was probably right, and he could agree with her. But at the same time he felt the need to comfort her, reassure her that she would be remembered. Kids always remembered those they idolized. Heck, he'd been a kid who worshiped cartoon superheroes.

Peter reached across the table and took her hand in his, but immediately regretted it. She stared at their hands then tugged to pull hers out of his grasp. "It's okay. I'm very aware that fame is fleeting. That's why I want to make sure that I have evergreen content."

His brows furrowed. "Evergreen?"

"You know, like the stuff that will hold up to the test of time? Baking is something people will keep doing even twenty years into the future. But not video games."

Peter chuckled. "You seriously don't think video games will be around?"

"Oh, they'll be around. But do you remember when the first video game station came out?" She snapped her fingers. "There was this game. I don't remember what it was called, but we had to hunt ducks."

His lips twitched, tugging into a knowing smile. "I think I know exactly what game you're referring to."

"Right." She smiled back. "Anyway, games today are nothing like that one. They're constantly evolving. I would bet that Kat wouldn't know the first thing about playing something like that, when there are VR options coming out."

She made an excellent point. Once again, he was blown away by her obvious intelligence. She wasn't just some air-headed, entitled brat. She was thinking about her future and willing to help him along the way. "So, you want to make videos about baking that will still be relevant in the future."

She nodded.

"Then may I make a suggestion?"

"Please do."

He had her undivided attention and it both terrified him and exhilarated him. "Whenever you're in the kitchen, use the most rudimentary tools. Make it simple for people who can't afford the newest gadget. Help people see they can get back to their roots when it comes to baking."

"I like that idea."

"Like what idea?" Kat returned to the table and scooted next to him. He wrapped his arm around her shoulders and pressed a kiss to her temple. "*Father*," she groaned.

"We're just talking about how I can make my videos more approachable." Quinne gave him a meaningful look. "Your dad's a pretty smart guy."

Kat craned her neck around and stared up at him. "Yeah, I guess he's alright."

Peter again mouthed the words 'thank you' to the woman he never thought he would need to thank. She was nothing like he expected, and he found he liked that a lot more than he probably should.

Quinne's gaze dipped to her lap, but he didn't miss the small smile that touched her lips. Maybe this arrangement of theirs wouldn't be so bad after all.

Chapter Nine

For what felt like the hundredth time, Quinne glanced over at Peter. The kitchen was quiet now that lunch had been taken care of. Kat had begged to go with some of her friends to a movie, which left Quinne alone with Peter.

It was probably a good thing she didn't have Kat underfoot. She needed to put together what she was going to do for her first video, which she planned on filming tomorrow. That was becoming increasingly more difficult the more time she spent in this room with a certain someone.

Dinner the other night had been a dream. She'd never thought she would enjoy spending time with someone like Peter—someone who was a little older than she normally went for, and who had a daughter, no less.

Sure, he was a little more serious than she preferred, too, but he had his moments.

A smile touched her lips and she had to turn her face so her shoulder hid it. She still couldn't believe that he'd agreed to an eating competition. There was just something about this guy that tugged at her heartstrings.

And she needed to shut it down.

Quinne gave her head a solid nod and turned to retrieve a scale she'd seen on a shelf behind her. At that very moment, Peter decided to pass behind her, causing her to collide with him and a pot of tepid water.

The liquid arced out of the pot in a wave which hit Quinne then came down with a smack against the tiled floor. Immediate warmth, followed quickly by cold, saturated her blouse and jeans. Quinne gasped; her hands spread out as she stared at the mess she'd become.

Laughter brought her attention upward. If it weren't for the fact that she was now chilled and wet, the way his eyes captured hers would have made her legs melt.

Oh, who was she kidding?

She was melting, just like the wicked witch in that movie.

His laughter was low and warm and all she could do was stare at him, her mouth hanging open. Time slowed to a standstill then sped up like a movie on fast-forward.

He placed the pot on the counter. "I'm so sorry. Are you okay?"

Her gaze shifted to her white blouse that now clung to her body. She crossed her arms and blushed. "I think I need a new shirt."

Peter sobered and averted his eyes. Could he get any more adorable? He gestured toward a tall cabinet. "I think I have a few spare shirts in there if you want to borrow one. They won't fit, but at least you won't be cold and wet."

Quinne's focus flitted to the cabinet and she backed away from him.

Bad move.

Her traction-less flats apparently hated her. With one step, she slipped on the wet floor. Arms flinging outward and eyes going wide, Quinne braced herself for impact.

Peter's hands shot out and grasped hers, pulling her upright and then against him.

All she could comprehend at this moment was that she had successfully avoided a concussion, but she was dangerously close to a heart attack. The beating in her chest continued wildly, despite the fact she'd been rescued. What felt like an infinite amount of time was really only a few moments.

Peter stepped back quickly but cautiously. "Slower this time. Watch the water." His hand remained tight around her wrist as he guided her around him and past the puddle on the floor. "And maybe get some new shoes for in here. Sturdier."

Quinne snorted. "I like my shoes." And maybe she liked being rescued more than she would ever admit. She shuffled toward the cabinet and flung it open, grabbing a shirt without looking too closely at it. "I'll change and be right back."

While she should have felt chilled in the kitchen, the exact opposite was in fact true. Her whole body felt flushed, heated from the inside out, and all over a two-minute interaction with a guy who probably still thought she was just some lazy internet sensation.

She couldn't get her heart to calm, nor could she

seem to get the blush to leave her cheeks. Quinne unbuttoned her blouse and draped it over a chair in the empty office she'd found. She held up the shirt she'd taken and paused. It was a white dress shirt and, even though it wasn't on her, she could smell his cologne. She'd have to roll up the sleeves and maybe tie the bottom together so it didn't drown her.

Her fingers traced over his name, which had been embroidered over the pocket. This shirt must be one he used just for work.

A quiet thrill rippled through her at the thought of wearing something of his. No manner of chastising herself could make her feel guilty enough about those thoughts.

A knock at the door drew her attention and she brought the shirt to her chest as she whirled around. "Yes?"

"You doing okay? Is that shirt going to work for you?" Peter's muffled voice was laced with laughter. Funny how she could hear said amusement even without looking at him directly.

"Yeah," she squeaked then cleared her throat. "Yes. It will be just fine."

"Do you want me to have someone in the laundry room throw your shirt into the dryer?"

"Absolutely not!" Quinne grimaced. Peter was a guy. He wouldn't understand that her shirt had to be dry cleaned. Most of her outfits had that requirement. Come to think of it, she probably needed to get a few new items for her wardrobe, if she wanted to get serious about cooking. "My shirt can't go through the dryer. I'll just hang it over a chair or something. Thanks anyway."

She wasn't certain, but she could have sworn he was still outside the door hovering. That knowledge was enough to make her fingers numb and uncooperative as she attempted to button up the shirt she had borrowed.

Peter's scent was all around her now, making it far more difficult to put herself back into the right kind of headspace. She couldn't exactly hide out in the office all day. She had to get everything prepped for the video tomorrow.

Quinne heaved a sigh as she pulled the two sides of Peter's shirt together and tied them in a knot just above the waistband of her jeans. She rolled the sleeves up to her elbows and let the collar hang open around her collarbone. There wasn't a mirror anywhere nearby, but at this point that shouldn't matter anyway.

She draped her wet shirt over her arm and exited the office. A mixture of relief and disappointment flooded her consciousness when she noted Peter's absence. He'd gone back to the kitchen. Or maybe he'd gone on his break.

Again, Quinne chastised herself for letting her thoughts wander back to the one guy she should probably stay away from.

Slipping down the hall and back into the kitchen, she continued repeating that she wasn't interested in dating right now, no matter how good he smelled or how cute his smile was.

But then he turned toward her, and those thoughts disappeared like the early morning fog on a chilly morning. His eyes swept over her form, lingering at her waist where she'd knotted the shirt to keep it from looking more like a dress. Part of her stomach was bare and for the first time in her life she felt exposed.

Quinne turned away from Peter, if only to avoid looking directly at him. She hooked her shirt on a hook near the door then moved through the kitchen, being sure to keep a certain amount of distance between them.

Without making eye contact, Quinne set back to work. Only, this time, she was far more aware of the other person in the room. Every time she felt his eyes on her, she got chills. It was tempting to unroll the sleeves just so she could cover the evidence of the goose bumps that ran rampant on her skin.

After a few minutes of focusing on her breathing and the recipe she had memorized by heart, she got back into the zone. Measure out the starter she had rehydrated. Add water and flour. By this time tomorrow, it would be fed, bubbly, and ready for making bread. There was just one problem. She needed several stages ready, so she'd be here longer than she expected. Quinne measured out the starter, flour and water then mixed them up and placed the jar aside. If everything went according to plan, she'd have some starter ready to mix into dough within about four hours.

Four freaking hours.

What was she supposed to do between now and then? Just sit in this kitchen while Peter the perfect prince peeled potatoes?

Quinne snickered and Peter glanced at her from where he hovered over the sink. His brows creased and his eyes narrowed. She ducked her head but couldn't hold back a second quiet laugh.

"Something funny?"

She nodded, then shook her head. "Just me being weird." Quinne had to turn away. Those eyes of his had a nasty habit of making her feel strange. It would probably be a good idea for her to leave the kitchen altogether. She could visit with her mother.

Oh, wait. Hadn't her mother's little group gone on another trip to town?

Well, if her mother was gone, she could just go home for a few hours.

But what if Kat came back from her movie and Peter needed Quinne's help?

She sighed again and leaned forward, her elbows resting on the metal countertop. Her options were to sit in the kitchen looking like an idiot or sitting out in the game room like one. If she'd been smart, she would have brought a book to read. But Quinne was never one to think ahead.

"You just gonna stand there?"

Her head snapped up and she stared at Peter. He gestured at her and her workspace with a potato peeler. "Because if you're just going to take up space, maybe you could make yourself useful."

Quinne straightened. "Sure. What do you need?" She wasn't sure if her response had surprised him or if it was something else, but Peter didn't answer her right away. When he finally seemed to come to, he held out his peeler. "Grab a few potatoes and peel them, then put them in this pot. I'm making warm potato salad with dinner tonight."

She grasped the peeler, and her fingers grazed against his. Peter's hand was a lot warmer than she'd expected. Whenever she was working in the kitchen, she usually ran a little colder—probably due to her hands constantly being washed.

Quinne froze in that position, her hand over the top of his as she had reached for the peeler. She stared at where they remained connected. Then he shifted, clearing his throat and she jumped back. Thankfully, she didn't lose her grip on the peeler and she could get right to work.

Peter retrieved a new peeler and resumed his task. "So, you're doing sourdough first?"

She nodded.

"What kind?"

Glancing up at him once more, she couldn't help but be surprised he had any interest in this topic at all. "Artisan."

He nodded. "That starter you're using—how old is it?"

Her lips quirked upward at the corners. "I hope you're not suggesting that I don't know what I'm doing. I assure you it's mature."

A smile graced his lips as he peeked at her before turning his attention back to the potato in his hand. "On the contrary. I haven't made sourdough bread in a long time. I thought maybe you'd share."

Her brows lifted. "You want some of my starter?"

"Would that be a problem?"

"Of course not. I'll have some discard in about three to four hours. You can take what you want of that."

"Thanks."

"I guess it makes sense." Her statement probably sounded like it came out of left field, but all he did was shoot a curious look in her direction. "That you know how to bake sourdough."

He chuckled. "Why is that?"

She motioned around the kitchen. "You singlehandedly handle all the cooking for this place five days a week. I haven't seen anyone helping out in the kitchen at all. I mean, sure, there are orderlies who take the food to everyone. But no one else cooking. It's really impressive."

Quinne didn't miss the fleeting smile of pride that flitted across his features.

"I do get a bit of help here and there, but thanks."

"You're welcome." Quinne shucked off some more potato skin, unable to keep her own smile from her face. This was nice and that fact couldn't have surprised her more than it did in that moment.

Chapter Ten

Peter was finding it harder and harder to concentrate. There was just something about seeing Quinne in part of his chef's uniform that had him feeling all turned inside out. He'd let his peeler slip on two occasions already, nearly cutting himself each time. If he wasn't careful, the residents were going to get something extra special in their potatoes for dinner tonight.

After she'd complimented him, he couldn't find anything to say that wouldn't sound absolutely weird. They were on two entirely separate planes of reality. He was ten years older than she was, divorced, a father. She lived in a world full of digital people and, as far as he could tell, her mother—who'd had Quinne late in her life—was her only relative. Her only responsibility.

They had zero in common.

Or at least, he'd thought they did.

Now he was discovering so much more about her.

Peter's interest had been piqued. He wanted to know more about her—spend more time with her. He could see now why his daughter was so enthralled with this woman.

There had to be a catch somewhere. No one was this perfect. No one was this selfless.

He peeked at her out of the corner of his eye. Then again, maybe someone was.

His hand slipped again, but this time the blade sliced all the way across the potato's skin and cut into his thumb. Peter sucked in sharply then muttered a string of expletives under his breath.

Quinne gasped, letting her potato and peeler clatter to the counter as she hurried toward him. He didn't know where she grabbed the towel from, but she jumped right into action, wrapping it around his hand and practically dragging him toward the sink. "How bad is it? Will you need stitches?"

She hovered over his hand, carefully unwrapping it from the towel before holding it under the running water.

He groaned, his teeth clenched from the stinging pain. Red mixed with the running water. The cut was deep but it shouldn't be too big. He'd barely caught himself. That's what he got for letting his focus drift from the task at hand.

Quinne made quick work of cleaning his thumb then wrapping it with a fresh towel. "Where's your first aid kit?" she demanded. He'd never heard her voice so firm before. "Peter. The first aid kit. Don't make me go hunting for it. You need to get this wrapped up right or it could get infected."

He motioned toward a little white box that hung on the wall. Quinne hurried toward it and dug out a few items. He wandered after her, the shock from the initial pain wearing off. “I’m sure it will be fine. I’ve had worse cuts before, I assure you.”

She shook her head. “It’s deep. I don’t think you should be—”

“Just get me a butterfly bandage for now and I’ll go and see nurse later if it gets worse.”

‘Nurse? Oh, the one on staff here? I can go find her.’

‘Rather you don’t. She’s busy enough with residents.’

“I have a friend who could stitch it up.”

Peter blinked at her. “You do?”

She nodded. “I took some nursing classes for a semester right out of high school before my influencer stuff took off—made some friends. I’m sure one of them could come out here and see if you need any special attention.” Before he could decline the offer, she had her phone out and then to her ear.

He rolled his eyes. “It’s not necessary—”

“Artie? I’m so glad I caught you. I thought for sure you’d be working.” Quinne held up a finger, cutting him off. “I know! It’s been forever. I’m so sorry I bailed on you when you wanted to go out.”

Go out? Was this Artie an ex? Had they dated?

Jealousy swirled within him stronger than he’d like to admit. Whoever this Artie was, Quinne had rebuffed his advances. That could work in Peter’s favor, right?

What favor?

He wasn’t supposed to be interested in her. It didn’t matter how much she’d impressed him. She wasn’t available to him for so many reasons.

Quinne laughed, drawing his attention. “Well, if you’re in the area, I was hoping you could help me out. I have a...” She glanced up at him then turned around so her back faced him. "... friend who inadvertently cut his hand while peeling potatoes. I'm not sure if we should put a stitch in it..." She laughed again. "You and I both know you could do it. Weren't you the one who said you chose to be a nurse over a doctor because you refused to bow to the establishment?"

Her laugh was getting to him. What made this guy so funny? Peter scowled, his hand tightening on the towel. At this rate, his thumb would be fully healed by the time this Artie showed up.

Peter stepped toward Quinne, prepared to tell her just that when she hung up the phone.

"Good news. Artie can be here soon. If it turns out you don't need anything but some extra bandage care, then at least we are better safe than sorry." She took his hand in hers. "Can I look at it?"

He tore his hand from her reach and shook his head. She had already done enough, namely got his heart pumping enough blood he was amazed he hadn't bled out already. Shaking his head again, he forced his voice to remain neutral. "I really wish you hadn't done that."

"Done what?"

"Called your friend. I was just fine. I didn't need any extra help."

She snorted. "You nearly sliced your thumb clean off. Maybe you should invest in some better peelers." Quinne glanced at the clock. "It's not gonna take long. Then you can get back to work and maybe aim for a less important digit."

"Ha. Ha. Funny." He muttered dryly.

Her lips twitched. "Glad to see your sense of humor hasn't completely disappeared." Expression sobering, she took another step toward him. "How is it feeling? Still stinging?"

"I told you it's fine." He held it out of reach. "How long until they get here?" He needed her to take a step back. Their proximity was making him light-headed—because it definitely wasn't his wound that was causing that reaction.

She pulled out her phone. "Soon."

"Would you mind working on those potatoes? I really need to get them boiling."

Quinne studied him. The way her gaze delved into his made him antsy. First the water incident. Then her nearly colliding with the floor, now this. He was beginning to wonder if this kitchen had become cursed.

Just when he thought she would ignore his request, she nodded and returned to her station. He cleaned up the mess from the cut. The quiet spread between them like an ominous mist. A lump formed in his throat—which was probably his only saving grace considering how much he wanted to ask her who this Artie was and where the guy stood in her life.

As much as he wanted to be logical about all of this, his heart rebelled. He didn't want to follow logic. He wanted to move closer to her, smell her hair, feel the warmth radiating from her skin. He wanted to know what made her tick.

A knock on the side of the door drew the attention of them both. Quinne stood from where she'd settled onto a stool. Olivia had her head poked through the doorway. Her eyes jumped from him to Quinne. "There's someone named Artie here to see you?" It was clear she didn't know what was going on by the way her focus continued to play ping-pong between them. "Do you want me to—"

"Send her in and thanks."

Wait a minute. Her?

Artie was a *woman*?

As if in answer to his query, a woman with curly black hair and green eyes materialized in the doorway. She and Quinne both squealed and closed the distance between the two of them, meeting halfway for a hug.

Peter released a breath that had been locked inside his chest. Artie wasn't a man after all. It was strange how the simple feeling of relief was enough to make him feel a hundred times better. He cleared his throat to get their attention and the two pulled apart.

Quinne gestured toward him. "Right. This is Peter. He's letting me use the kitchen for some of the new videos I'll be putting out. Peter, this is Artie."

He moved forward, holding out his right hand. "Artie. That's an unusual name."

Artie and Quinne exchanged looks and then laughed, before Artie accepted his offered hand. "Yeah. My parents thought they were doing me a favor, naming me something unique. Little did they know that Artemis was such a terrible choice."

His brows shot up. "Are you sure about that?"

She placed a hand on her hip. "You try living with the name of a blue messenger god from a childhood cartoon during your formative years and tell me how it goes." Her tone was light, but it was clear she wasn't thrilled with her given name. Not missing a beat, she motioned to his hand. "Let me see what's going on there." She didn't even wait before she grabbed his left hand and unwrapped it. "Good thing Quinne caught me. I'm taking an overdue vacation tomorrow so you'd have had to drag yourself to the nurse here.'

Artie made a face then pulled his hand closer to get a better look. It was still bleeding enough to need the towel wrapped around it once more.

"Yeah. You might be better off with at least one stitch. You got supplies?'

"Supplies? You mean like—"

She laughed, slicing her hand through the air. "Just kidding. I've got some stuff in my car. I'll be right back."

When she'd disappeared, he whirled around to face Quinne. "Are all of your friends so..." He couldn't come up with a word to describe her that wouldn't sound offensive. Boy, he wasn't on his best game today.

"Loud?" Quinne offered. She laughed, leaning against one of the counters as she crossed her arms. "I think I actually attract the loud ones. I don't know what it is. Maybe we're just peas in a pod, you know?"

Before he had a chance to put his foot in his mouth, Artie returned with a small black box. She tugged Peter over to a clear counter then dug through her stuff. Her lower lip puckered and she tilted her head. "You know what? I changed my mind. It'd just be easier if we do glue. It's gonna sting like all get out, but at least we won't have to wait for the stitch to dissolve." She flashed him a smile. "Besides, I don't have any numbing cream. This will be a lot better."

He grimaced. "Sting? Can't I just use a butterfly bandage or something?"

"I mean, you could. But it probably wouldn't stay like you're hoping. You use your hands a lot. I say let's clean it, then close it up. It'll heal faster that way too."

Artie was right.

The glue *burned*.

He cursed under his breath, which only caused the girls to smirk at one another. Apparently he hadn't been quiet enough when he'd used his colorful language.

Once the gluing and bandaging were done, he pulled on some fresh gloves and got right back to work.

Artie and Quinne chatted by the door for about five minutes, catching up. Quinne promised they'd have a get-together and this time she wouldn't bail.

He only caught snippets of their conversation—none of it making much sense. But he'd long since given up on staying in with the cool crowd.

Artie slipped out the door and Quinne returned to her station. She glanced up at him as she grabbed the potato and peeler. "Sorry about that."

"About what? Dragging your nurse friend here to help?"

She bit back a smile, then wiped at her face with her upper arm. "No. I'm sorry we sorta took over your kitchen. I know how you can be."

"It's fine," he muttered. "I guess I should thank you. At least now I know I won't be needing a tetanus shot."

Quinne's smile deepened. "The night is still young. Don't give up on your dreams quite yet."

He couldn't help the grin that crept onto his own face at her words. Okay, so she could make him smile. That didn't mean anything. He still needed to maintain a professional relationship, no matter how insurmountable that task might seem.

Chapter Eleven

Quinne dropped her keys onto the side table by the front door when she got back to her apartment. Today had been far more taxing than she'd anticipated. Part of her was ready to fall into bed and just close her eyes and welcome the oblivion of sleep.

But there was another part of her secretly counting down the hours until she was going to see Peter again. Dang it, she was acting just like a teenager. If she liked him so much, why couldn't she just ask him out?

Because he was technically her boss.

No, he wasn't. He wasn't paying her anything to watch his daughter. She'd offered that in exchange for his kitchen and access to said daughter.

A twinge of guilt slipped in among all the glee that had fueled her evening. As much as she'd convinced herself that she didn't need Kat for her videos, deep down she had to admit, the kid had a talent for pointing out certain aspects that Quinne might otherwise overlook. Eventually, she wanted to give Kat the opportunity to get out from behind the camera.

Peter had to be okay with that eventually, right? She'd win his trust and then she'd be able to help him see that being on camera wasn't all that bad. Nothing had happened to her in all the years she'd been active on social media.

She wandered to her room and fell back on her bed to stare at the ceiling. Peter was a down-to-earth kind of guy. More and more, she could see that part of him clearly. He wasn't like the guys in her social circles—spending some time with Artie had confirmed that.

The guys they'd hung around back when Quinne was still taking courses seemed to be in a standstill in their own lives. Artie couldn't name one man that Quinne had dated who had made something of himself.

That thought was disappointing.

More than disappointing, it bordered on embarrassing. These people were supposed to be the demographic that brought in the most change for the world. She'd hoped to see more from her peers. Quinne sighed and rolled to her side. Maybe realizing that had been the one thing that pushed her over the edge when it came to how she felt about Peter. He wasn't like anyone she'd dated. In fact, he was probably too good for her and she needed to set her sights on something—someone—more attainable.

That didn't mean they couldn't be friends, right?

Right.

"My dad said you were a fast thinker and if it weren't

for you, he might have had to go to the emergency room."

"*Kat*," Peter muttered with exasperation in his voice. His eyes flitted up to meet Quinne's and she chuckled.

"I'm glad I could help. Guys can be such wimps, you know?"

"Hey."

Quinne laughed again. "No offense. I just meant that I haven't met a single guy in my life who would willingly go to an urgent care unless he had a woman practically pushing him through the front door."

His eyes locked with hers and she could only hold his gaze for a moment before she couldn't take it. She broke their connection and motioned toward where they were going to be working today. "I brought my camera. How is the starter looking?"

Kat hurried over to where Quinne had left the container she'd set out the day before. Her eyes widened. "It's got bubbles."

"That's great." Quinne could feel Peter's eyes on her as she walked around the counter toward Kat. After she'd returned home last night, she didn't get much sleep. There was a battle going on in her head, namely that she had found herself attracted to him but knew better than to complicate the arrangement they had. Avoiding his gaze right now was even harder than giving in to the exhaustion she felt.

"Why do you want bubbles?"

Quinne dropped down to Kat's level and pointed at the jar. "Those bubbles show that it's fermenting. There are gases that will help our bread rise. It's a whole big science experiment."

Kat wrinkled her nose. "Science? That sounds boring."

Laughing, Quinne's eyes cut to Peter. Her heart stammered and she felt locked in place by his serious gaze. It was as if something passed between them, connecting them even stronger than before. Her heart was trying to communicate with him.

Peter cleared his throat, ending the strange enchantment she could have sworn she'd experienced. Quinne blinked a few times and focused on her breathing. That had to be the weirdest experience she'd had so far.

"What was I saying?"

"You were telling her that cooking can be like science," Peter's quiet voice broke through her defenses and she glanced at him once more. "You were saying the starter had chemical reactions in it that caused those bubbles."

"Right." She turned to Kat and traced her finger along the side of the jar. "What's really cool is that the longer you let this sit, the more bubbly it will become. But if you don't feed it, it will eventually die."

"You *feed* it? Like a pet?"

Quinne grinned. "Exactly. There are even some people who name their starter for that very reason." She put herself on autopilot, teaching Kat about the nuances involved in cooking with starter and finally was able to break away from the hold Peter had on her.

They set up the camera and Kat's features scrunched as she stared at it.

"What's the matter?"

She glanced up at Quinne. "Don't you do these things live?"

"Sometimes. But right now, I'm reworking my platform. I want to have several videos to put out all at once." She nudged Kat playfully. "Your generation is so impatient. I have to have stuff ready to go right out of the gate or they might not come back. That's how you hook 'em."

It was harder than she thought it would be, talking to the camera with Peter in the room. Her first couple of takes, she was flustered and had to restart. Several times she blushed and had to turn around to prevent anyone from noticing.

Something was off with her and she couldn't figure out what it was.

Okay, she was lying to herself. She knew exactly what the problem was, and he was standing a few feet away from her.

By the time the recording part was done, she had wisps of hair that had fallen out of her ponytail, her face was hot, and her hands tingled from all the fidgeting. She attempted to avoid looking at Peter but failed miserably. Stolen glances were just going to have to be the norm for now.

At some point Peter dug out his phone then handed it over to Kat. "I think Chelsey is calling you."

Kat took the phone from him and answered, moving out of the room.

How did the kitchen suddenly seem so much smaller after one person *left*? Quinne turned her back to Peter, hoping that it would help settle her nerves if she wasn't able to see him.

It didn't.

Every breath he took, every shuffle of his feet against the tile, she heard it all. To top it off, her ears had to be playing tricks on her because she kept thinking he was closer than he was. She picked up the camera and swept through the footage. Seven starts. For goodness's sake. She was supposed to be a professional. One retake was acceptable, but seven? Kat burst into the kitchen, causing Quinne to nearly jump out of her skin.

"Dad! Chelsey said I could come over. She got a new video game and she wants me to play it with her."

Peter met Quinne's eyes briefly and she shrugged though her insides were still running a hundred miles a minute. "I'm here to keep an eye on her either way. I have some cleaning up to do and then I was going to check in with my mom."

Kat groaned. "Please, Dad! I don't get to hang out with her that much."

His jaw tightened, but it was fleeting. He stood at the sink washing carrots for today's meal. With a swift motion, he shut off the water. "Are her parents going to be home?"

"I don't *know*. We're old enough to be alone, though. We won't do anything stupid. I promise."

Peter arched a brow and Quinne bit back a smile behind her shoulder. Raising a daughter wasn't easy and if Kat was anything like Quinne, he didn't know what he had coming.

He took a few steps toward his daughter and placed his hands on her shoulders. "You call me if anything happens."

She let out a squeal. "Really?"

"I'm going to regret this, aren't I?" he murmured.

Kat shook her head, bouncing on the balls of her feet. Her hair bounced around her shoulders as she shook her head. "No, you won't. I promise." She looked toward Quinne and squealed again. "I'm going to tell her all about what we did today. This is going to be awesome!"

"How are you going to get there?"

Without missing a beat, Kat picked up the phone she'd left on the counter and brought it to her ear. "Your brother can come get me."

"Wait, her *brother*?" Peter shot one more look in Quinne's direction and followed his daughter out of the kitchen.

Finally, she could breathe.

Quinne rested both palms on the metal counter and dipped her chin to her chest. She'd dated before. She'd had crushes before. Each one was different and fun, but no one had ever affected her like this. Her heart felt like it had run a marathon all on its own, while her lungs ached from when she'd been holding her breath. This wasn't normal.

"Get your act together," she muttered.

"What?"

Quinne jumped backward and bumped against a rolling table behind her. Plastic bowls and cups clattered to the floor and once again her face was in bloom. "I'm so sorry!" She stammered, dropping to the floor to gather the fallen dishes. "I wasn't looking—I didn't realize—"

He rounded the counter, chuckling. "It's fine. We've all bumped into that table at one point or another." His hand brushed hers when they reached for the same cup and she jerked backward as if a snake had bitten her. Peter gave her a funny look, gathered the stacked dishes and got to his feet. "You think you have everything figured out and then you get knocked to the ground again."

Her wide eyes fluttered. "What?" Had he noticed the way she was acting around him? She didn't think he looked very upset, but what did she know?

Peter crossed his arms, leaning back against the counter as he glanced at her once more. "It feels like yesterday that Kat started kindergarten."

Quinne exhaled, releasing the breath that had been caught in her chest. "Oh."

"Now, she's growing up and she doesn't need me anymore."

She snorted. "Kat will always need you. There's no question about that."

Peter eyed her, a crooked grin on his face. "Sure doesn't seem that way. She didn't even want me to wait with her for her ride."

Quinne sliced her hand through the air dismissively. "She's getting to an age where dads aren't 'cool', but she will never stop needing you." She pressed her lips together, emotion rising. "I wish my dad was still around. I'd give anything to get one of his hugs again."

He blinked. "I'm so sorry."

She let out a watery laugh. "He's been gone ten years. But I still miss him. Kat's just going through a phase. You'll see."

Peter turned around and rested his forearms on the metal countertop. "You're really good with her, you know."

Quinne went stock-still. She hadn't seen the conversation going in this direction. She glanced at him sideways, moving into a similar position beside him. A smile tugged at her lips. "Didn't I say I'm good with kids?"

"I suppose you're right." They stayed like that for a few moments and the longer the silence stretched, the harder her heart thundered. She was sure he could hear it clear as day. "Well, you're going to be a wonderful mother."

His words sent chills scattering through her body. Every single nerve ending was on fire and she couldn't bring herself to look him in the eye. That statement alone shouldn't have affected her at all, and yet she found herself reading into it more than she should. She tucked a wisp of hair behind her ear and let out a strained laugh. "Thanks." It was all she could think of saying. Her eyes dropped to his hand where his thumb now only had a plaster. "How is your hand? Is it okay?"

Peter wiggled his thumb. "I've had worse." He twisted so his hip rested against the counter and he faced her. She could feel his eyes drilling into her. Part of her knew that if she met his gaze she'd be trapped. That would be a very bad idea. And yet she went against everything her head told her not to do.

Quinne turned her head so her chin rested on her shoulder. Peter opened his mouth. Shut it. Then shook his head. "Kat will probably spend the rest of the day with her friend. You don't need to be here anymore."

Her heart sank and she didn't even have a good reason for that happening. Peter scooped the dishes into his arms and brushed past her. Was he asking her to leave? Because that's what it felt like.

Chapter Twelve

"I'm sorry, did I do something wrong?"

Peter glanced over his shoulder after he deposited the dishes in the sink. "What? No. Why?"

She closed the distance between them. From the way she walked, to the crease between her brows, he could tell something was bothering her.

Well, that was fine, because something was bothering him, too. He hadn't been able to stop thinking about her. He blamed it on seeing her every day, but it was more than that. She haunted his dreams. On more than one occasion thoughts of her distracted him. He'd cut his thumb because he'd allowed himself to get distracted. What next? He couldn't afford to damage any other appendages.

He crossed his arms, reminding himself this was how lawsuits happened. He'd become infatuated with her. There was no denying it now, but acting on those feelings would only stir up trouble.

"You told me to leave."

His brows lifted. "No, I didn't."

"Yes, you did. You said I didn't need to be here anymore."

He glanced around the kitchen. "That's because this is my workplace. You're the one crashing it. I still don't know how this is going to help Isaac out. You're just taking up space." Inwardly, he flinched. He actually liked her company, but he needed a way to maintain the distance that seemed to be crumbling with each passing hour. If he wasn't careful, he'd end up doing something really stupid.

His eyes dipped to her lips as if agreeing with that sentiment. He'd wondered what a kiss might taste like, how she'd feel in his arms, but he was better than that. He refused to put either of them in an uncomfortable position.

Her mouth fell open and her cheeks flushed that pretty pink color he'd seen several times today. Several emotions battled it out across her features. She looked adorable. Finally, she took in a deep breath and let it out. "Whatever it was I did, I'm sorry. I'll try to stay out of your hair from now on."

Quinne turned on her heel to walk away. His hand shot out as if he intended to grab her and pull her close, but he restrained himself. What was he doing?

Peter spun around and grasped the edge of the sink with both hands. He glowered into the pile of dishes that were there and berated himself for his weakness. All it would take was one complaint and he could risk losing his job. Heck, he'd seen the way society pounced on men who chased after what they wanted. These days all it took was one video on social media and the man was crucified.

This was better. Hands off and creating distance no matter how much he wanted something else.

Behind him Quinne gasped. He turned around in time to see her holding her pointer finger.

"What happened?" he demanded.

Her expression remained cool, but her tone indicated just how unhappy she was with him. "It's just a nick."

Peter grabbed her hand to examine it. She was right, it was a superficial wound. He looked around, finding the source of her injury. He grabbed the bread knife and lifted it up.

She nodded. "I was checking to see if it would work for what I needed."

"And what was that? Chopping off your finger?"

Quinne tore her hand from his. "Excuse me, but out of the two of us, you're the one who needed medical assistance. Mine is no worse than a papercut."

"A papercut that's bleeding."

"Then a papercut from cardboard," she shot back. "I just need a Band-Aid and it will be fine by tomorrow. What do you want me to say? I'll be more careful, okay?" She muttered something under her breath that he didn't understand as she strode away from him.

He put the knife with the rest of the washing up and told himself that she was right and he shouldn't push the issue.

There was only one problem. He wasn't in a good headspace right now and there was a part of him that refused to listen to reason. "You're my responsibility."

She stopped, her hand mid-air as she reached for the first aid kit.

"Isaac might have cleared you for this, but I'm still

the one in charge. If anything happens to you, I'm liable."

Her hand dropped and she faced him. "You're not seriously giving me a lecture over this."

"I agreed to let you use the kitchen to *cook*. Not once did you say you would be slicing your hand open."

She tossed her head back with a huff. "That's rich coming from a guy who nearly cut off his whole thumb. Fine. I'll get my things and get out of your hair." Quinne stormed through the kitchen, yanking her jacket and purse into her arms. She didn't meet his gaze even once before leaving the room.

Peter exhaled. It was for the best. He'd felt cornered by these emotions that continued to grow—emotions he couldn't act on. He'd have to figure out how to make this work when Kat was back. For now, Quinne needed to be off the premises.

Peter's phone buzzed in his pocket. He glanced at the clock on the wall. Too soon for Kat to want to be picked up. When he retrieved his phone, he didn't recognize the number. He frowned, contemplating letting it go to voicemail, but changed his mind at the last second.

"Hello?"

"Peter Edmonds?"

"Yes? Who is this?"

"My name is Officer Tad Jeffries. There's been an accident."

Peter stiffened. "What happened? Is my daughter—"

"I have Ms. Hart's phone here and you were her

most recent contact. We tried the number named 'Mom' but it rang out."

His heart stopped and the blood drained from his face. "Is she all right?" he demanded. "What happened?" he repeated.

"You know her?"

"She—" He caught himself. Would this officer give him any information if he didn't claim to know her well? To say she worked for him might shut this conversation down before he could figure out what had happened. Peter cleared his throat. "She's my fiancée." Quinne didn't need to know any of this. From what he knew, she didn't have any other family who they could call anyway. Her mother lived at Maple Gardens and before distressing Alice, he should get some details. It was possible she had a sibling, but he'd never seen anyone else visit Alice. "Can I speak to her?"

"I'm sorry, that's not possible at the moment. She was taken to the hospital—"

Peter grabbed his keys and jacket. "Which one?"

"She'll be fine, they just wanted to check her out for any internal injuries."

His stomach twisted, knotted and churned to the point he couldn't breathe. "I don't need an update on her vitals, I'll get that at the hospital. Where did they take her?"

"Sweet Haven on Tenth."

"I'm going there now." Peter hung up the phone without waiting for the officer to say anything else. Officer Jeffries would likely head to the hospital for a statement anyway. Peter's priority was making sure Quinne was okay.

Peter darted through the sliding glass doors and right up to the emergency room reception. "Quinne Hart," he demanded. "Where is she?"

The startled nurse peered at him for a moment then turned to her computer. "Are you related to the patient?"

"I'm her fiancé. Peter." Strange how it was getting easier to say that out loud. At least no one questioned him when he sounded so confident. He dropped both hands onto the counter. "Her mom is in an assisted living home. Quinne's been in an accident. She needs me and I'm not leaving until I make sure she's okay."

Hesitation flickered over her expression and she glanced to another nurse at a nearby computer. The other woman gave her a short nod. The nurse returned her gaze to Peter's and she let out a sigh. "I'll have security escort you. She's in room 2A." She motioned toward a man standing near a door that led to what was probably a hallway. "Stan will take you."

Peter rushed forward, his steps quick. He didn't know how Quinne would react to him showing up. Hopefully she wouldn't give him away, because he didn't know how the security guy would react to hearing he had lied. Peter would have to worry about that later. Right now he needed to make sure she was okay. That was all.

The security guy stopped in front of a room that was closed off with a curtain.

"I told you, I'm fine. I don't need to be admitted. I'm not nauseous. I just need to go home and get some sleep."

"I'm afraid that's not possible. You need to be monitored. You have a concussion."

"I told you, I feel fine." Her words were followed immediately by a gagging sound and shuffling.

Peter flinched on hearing the sound of someone being sick. He glanced at his security escort who gestured toward the curtain. "Well? Aren't you going to go in?"

Pulling aside the curtain, Peter slipped into the emergency room to find Quinne on the edge of the examination table with a butterfly bandage on her forehead. Her eyes shifted to him the moment he entered the room and surprise flickered across her face.

The doctor standing beside her with a tablet in his hands glanced over to him, then to Quinne. "I'm sorry, but it's policy right now that only family can visit."

"He's my brother," Quinne blurted.

Peter froze. Dang it, that would have been a better excuse. He only prayed that the security guy in the hall had already walked away.

The doctor's focus shifted from Quinne to Peter and back again. "Like I was saying, we're going to have to admit you for monitoring. You said you didn't live with anyone. So there is no one who can keep an eye on you. If your symptoms worsen, then you wouldn't have the ability to get here."

"She can stay with me." Peter didn't know what prompted him to offer such a thing. It was as if his heart had gone rogue. This was a bad idea—a *very* bad idea.

But it would only be for one night. He could handle one night, especially if it helped him get back on Quinne's good side.

He cleared his throat, stepping forward. "I'll arrange for someone to work my shift tonight and tomorrow and I have room at my place. Just let me know what I need to look for and I'll do it." Peter could feel Quinne's eyes on him, which only caused his insides to revolt. His stomach turned inside out and his heart raced. If he wasn't careful, the doctor might have to hook him up to some of this machinery.

The doctor considered his offer then turned to Quinne. "That would be a reasonable alternative."

Peter finally chanced a look in her direction. Her mouth hung open, but she only kept his gaze a moment before she shifted her focus to the doctor. "Okay. I'll do it."

"You can set up an appointment with your primary care physician within the next couple of days. If you show any signs of distress you need to come in right away." The doctor turned to Peter. "I'll have a packet printed up for your reference. Contrary to popular belief, she doesn't need to be woken up every hour or two hours. You just need to keep tabs on her vitals. I'll give her some nausea medication. If she can't keep anything down or she becomes lethargic, don't hesitate to bring her in right away."

This was actually happening. He was inviting a woman into his home—a woman he wasn't married to—a woman who he found incredibly attractive.

Dang it.

What had he done?

Chapter Thirteen

Quinne fidgeted in the passenger seat of Peter's car. This whole situation was surreal. It couldn't be happening. For the first time in her life she wished she wasn't an only child. She wished she had a better relationship with her parents. And she wished that she hadn't left Maple Gardens so distracted.

To be fair, she'd been distracted because of the man seated beside her—so distracted she hadn't noticed the car running the red light when hers turned green.

She groaned, letting her head fall back against the headrest. Her car was likely totaled. At least that's what the officer had said when he arrived just before they released her.

Peter shifted in his seat. "You feeling okay? Do I need to pull over?"

She peeked at him out of the corner of her eye. "I'm fine. I don't even understand why they wouldn't just let me go home. I'm more than capable of calling for help if something went wrong."

He snorted.

Quinne shot him a sharp look. "What?"

Peter shook his head. "Nothing."

"That wasn't nothing. You don't think I can take care of myself, do you? I bet you think I'm just like a child. Well, I'll tell you something—"

He jerked the wheel to the side and they swerved off the road. Her heart leaped into her chest and she clawed at her seat, muttering a curse.

"Don't you get it?" he ground out, as he pulled to a stop. "There is a reason your doctor said you couldn't handle being home alone and it's not because you're clearly incapable of accepting when you need help. It's because if he sent you home in your state and something bad happened, he could be sued. Do you have any concern for others? Or do you only care for yourself?" He threw his hands into the air and let out a sigh. "That's not even the half of it. People care about you, Quinne."

She stilled, her heart still coming off the high of that sudden departure from the road. His tone of voice sent chills rippling through her body. It wasn't that she disagreed with him, but she definitely wouldn't be the first to admit he made a good point. She was far too stubborn for that.

Even still, as the echo of his words filled the silence between them, she couldn't help but feel guilty for what had happened. It still wasn't clear how he'd found out where she was or how he'd managed to get past the front desk.

Quinne clasped her hands in her lap, mumbling the only thing that came to her mind. "I'm sorry."

Peter glanced at her, though he didn't speak right away.

The tension continued to grow, expanding until it filled the car with its weight. She felt suffocated, unable to move. "Thank you for coming."

At first she didn't think he'd respond. It was as if this evening's events had siphoned all the energy he'd had in his reserves. Then he let out a sigh. "You're welcome."

Her gaze cut to meet his. "What are you going to tell Kat? She's bound to notice that I'm staying with you."

"We'll tell her the truth."

Quinne grimaced. "I don't know if that's a good idea."

"Why not? It's not like the accident was your fault."

Technically, it was. If she'd looked before putting her foot on the gas, she might have been able to avoid the collision altogether. But she knew what he meant. The one who was in trouble was the guy who'd been looking at his phone when he ran the red light. She'd been incredibly lucky that she'd walked away with only a scratch—and a beat-up car.

Peter gave her one final look before he put his car into drive and merged back into traffic. "I'll make us some dinner and then I'll check in with Kat. Her friend lives close enough to my place that you wouldn't have to be home alone for long when I get her."

Flutters erupted in her chest, consuming her insides and making her stomach churn all over again. She was going to be at Peter's home. What was she thinking? Things were tense enough without the two of them being in such close proximity. Quinne's grip on her hands tightened. She was going to be on her best behavior, so he wouldn't regret saving her from the clutches of that dreadful hospital.

After a quick stop at her place to pick up a few things, it wasn't long before Peter pulled into a little gate that led to a gated community. The homes weren't extravagant. Her eyes bounced from house to house as they went farther into the neighborhood. It was a cute place—the kind that stories were told about. "I don't believe it," she muttered.

Peter glanced in her direction. "What?"

She pointed out the window. "There is literally a white picket fence around that house."

He gave her a funny look. "Yeah, there is."

Quinne settled back in her seat with a sigh. "I can't believe you are one of *those* people."

One brow lifted and he chuckled. "One of *those* people? What's that supposed to mean?"

"You know. The guy with the house, the kid... the white picket fence," she drawled. "Let me guess. You have a puppy, too."

He wrinkled his nose. "Actually, I'm allergic."

She let out an exaggerated gasp. "How *devastating*."

The amusement was still written all over his face. "Well, what about you?"

"What *about* me?" she countered.

"I saw your place. If you were a guy, that apartment would be the ultimate bachelor pad."

Quinne shrugged. Her place was nice, there was no denying it. But it was lonely—unless she had friends over. Most of the people she could call friends weren't really that friendly. She wasn't an idiot. Generally speaking, people only spent time with her when they wanted something. That was the cost of fame. "It's not as great as it seems."

He glanced at her sideways. "Not that great? It's a little slice of paradise. Granted, you could do with a better kitchen—especially seeing as you're trying to redo your social media platform—but other than that, you're pretty lucky."

She rubbed her hands up and down her arms. To the outside world, she had the perfect life. She had fame, followers, money, and a nice place to live. But although she spent some time with her mother, Alice had her own friends at Maple Gardens and Quinne didn't have any other family or a close-knit support system. Even Artie wasn't as close to her these days. One more peek at Peter and she had to admit he was probably the closest thing she had to a friend.

The house they stopped at was exactly what she'd expected based on what she'd seen in the neighborhood already. The lawn was so perfectly manicured it could have been a scene in an edition of *Better Homes and Gardens* magazine.

There was only one thing she noticed that set this house apart from the others. Where the houses on either side of Peter's had roses or ornamental shrubs, Peter had a pear tree and what appeared to be an herb garden.

Quinne got out of Peter's car, and her eyes locked on the plants growing near the front door. He definitely had an herb garden and she recognized basil, cilantro, and chives at first glance.

She heard his footsteps behind her and she glanced over her shoulder toward him. "I don't believe it."

The corners of his mouth twitched. "What?"

"You have an herb garden. In the front yard. Isn't there some kind of rule about what you can and can't plant? Don't you have to follow guidelines or something in this neighborhood?"

He chuckled. "As long as my yard looks like it's taken care of, I can plant whatever I want." Peter jerked his chin toward the house. "Come on. Let's get you off your feet. I don't need you passing out and getting another concussion on my watch."

She wrinkled her nose as she got to her feet. "I'm fine and I don't need you bossing me around."

"Yes, ma'am." He gave her a small salute before he moved past her to open the door.

Quinne rolled her eyes and shuffled after him. "You can be kinda annoying."

"What? *Me*?"

"Yeah, you."

"Speak for yourself." His muttered words might have been construed as harsh if it wasn't for his soft expression. Once again, the chaotic beating in her chest resumed with a vengeance, just like when he'd told her people cared about her. She hadn't missed the way his tone of voice seemed to weigh more heavily on that sentence. If he hadn't meant for her to assume he was part of that group of people, then he shouldn't have said what he did.

Quinne followed him farther into the house. He tossed his keys on a table near the door and they moved through a sitting area toward an arched walkway. The house opened up beyond that to a huge kitchen that appeared to be half of the main level. One whole wall was filled with cabinets and sweeping countertops. Pendant lights hung over an expansive island and there were two stove tops that she could see. This kitchen put hers to shame. No wonder Peter had mentioned hers needed a face-lift.

"Wow," she breathed, "this is amazing." She moved forward as if she were no longer in control of her own legs. Her fingers traced over the quartz countertops with reverence. Peter was right. She could have done with a better kitchen. His home had a hidden gem within it and a sudden burst of envy ripped through her with a vengeance. "How did you..."

He chuckled, leaning casually against a stainless steel, restaurant-quality refrigerator. "It didn't come with the house, if that's what you're asking. I had it put in after we moved here. I can give you the number of my guy if you'd like to redo yours."

Her gaze flitted to meet his. "I might have to take you up on that."

Peter pushed away from the fridge, then pulled it open. "What are you in the mood for? I've probably got anything you might be interested in eating."

"I doubt that," she laughed. "Just make whatever you were planning on having already."

"What, you think I'm lying?" He glanced at her over his shoulder.

"*No*, I think you have a big head and too much confidence. I'm going to let you save face, because there is no way you have all the ingredients for what I am actually craving."

He turned to face her fully. "Try me."

"Okay, how about tempura shrimp and imitation crab sushi that is dipped in tempura and topped with unagi?"

Peter stared at her and she smirked. She knew he

couldn't possibly have that stuff on hand. Anyone who did was either really into sushi or...

Her eyes widened when he stepped over to open the freezer. "I have everything you need, but we're going to have to defrost some of it. Luckily, I have them frozen in small portions." He glanced at her, a grin stretched across his face. "Kat doesn't eat fish. But you probably could have predicted that."

Her mouth hung open. "You're kidding."

"No, she really doesn't like fish."

She stepped forward, shaking her head. "You know that's not what I'm talking about. You can't possibly have everything we need to make sushi—like the restaurants do."

Peter arched a brow. "I'm a chef who enjoys eating. I'm going to have most things." He gestured around the kitchen. "I mean, look at this place. It would be a complete waste if I couldn't use it the way it was intended."

"I guess you're right," she mumbled.

Chapter Fourteen

Peter scooped out the rice that had cooled while he'd prepared everything else for their sushi night then glanced at Quinne out of the corner of his eye. She sat at the bar, watching with lidded eyes. She looked totally exhausted.

"You should go sit on the couch and I'll finish this."

She shook her head even as she yawned. "Not on your life, buddy. I want to see how you dip that whole thing in the tempura and fry it."

He smiled. "At the rate you're going, you're gonna end up unconscious on my counter. How about I promise to teach you my special techniques?"

Quinne eyed him with what could only be suspicion. "You don't like me working in the kitchen with you. I doubt you'd be willing to teach me a dang thing."

Peter let out a laugh. "Where did you get a crazy idea like that?"

She held up her finger. "Your honor, I present exhibit A." There was a Band-Aid wrapped around the tip of the finger she'd nicked while they'd been at Maple Gardens.

Chagrined, he made a face. "In my defense, I had thought we might be needing another visit from your friend."

"Hey, my friend is the one who saved you," she muttered indignantly. "And this was just a flesh wound." She nodded toward what he was working on. "How do you get the rice to be so sticky? I can never get mine to behave like that."

"You probably don't have the right type of rice. Certain brands have more starch, which helps."

"Oh."

He pushed the mat with the rice and seaweed toward her. "How about you fill this one."

The smile that immediately graced her face did something to him. His stomach tightened and a shiver rumbled through him. The way she could brighten a room with one look was next level. No wonder she'd become so popular on her social media channel.

Watching her videos was fun, but having her here in person was even better. He watched as she placed cut up portions of avocado, crab, and cream cheese on the roll then added a few pieces of shrimp. Her eyes bounced up to meet his with excitement as she set to work rolling the rice. Only she wasn't rolling it tight enough to lock everything in.

He shook his head and walked around the island. "You need to do it tighter, otherwise it's just going to fall apart when we fry it. Here, like this." His arms came around her, and his hands covered hers as he demonstrated how to make a tight roll.

Quinne's hands were cool to the touch, but soft. Her

hair smelled floral and sweet. When she shifted, he became acutely aware of how close they were. She turned her head slightly and he could feel her breath on his cheek where he leaned over her shoulder.

Peter's heart leaped into his chest and all the feelings that had been slowly invading him came rushing to the surface. She tugged one hand free from his, placing it on his cheek. Her feathery touch grazed the five o'clock shadow that had sprouted on his jawline.

Her breathing sounded shallower, matching his own. His pulse raced and his whole body went on high alert, the sushi forgotten.

Quinne turned on her stool, facing him. Her face tilted upward and her legs enfolded him where he stood. The blood in his ears roared and something in his head screamed at him to just go for it. There was nothing to hold him back. She clearly wanted *something* from him. Who was he to disappoint her?

He hooked a finger under her chin, then grasped it as if doing so would prevent her from escaping. She exhaled breathily and her eyes fluttered closed. He wanted this. He wanted it more than he had thought possible.

And yet there was something holding him back. She had just been in a stressful situation.

Peter dropped his hand and took a swift step backward. He cleared his throat as he marched around the island to return to his spot. He avoided looking directly at her because he knew if he did, he wouldn't be able to control himself.

He heard her shift again, the sound of her feet hitting the tile seeming to echo in his kitchen. Good.

They both needed to take a break to think about what they'd nearly done.

Only she didn't leave the kitchen. Her footsteps rounded the counter and she shoved his shoulder.

He jumped and chanced a glance toward her. "What?"

"Don't *what* me."

Peter placed both hands on the counter, focusing on his breathing. Her proximity was getting to him. "You need to rest and I need to finish our meal."

"To heck with that."

His jaw tightened, defenses rising. "You were in an accident. It's normal for you to latch onto the closest—"

"How *dare* you." She let out a groan. "You can't even bother to look at me, can you?"

Slowly, he faced her. "You need to rest," he repeated.

"So you said."

"After you get some sleep, you'll realize this is a very bad idea."

Quinne glowered at him. "What does that even mean? Do you think something bad will happen if you kiss me?" Her cheeks burst with color, but she kept her eyes locked on him.

"I *know* something bad will happen."

"That's ridiculous! It's just a kiss."

Peter bristled. He raked a hand through his hair and let out a huff. "A kiss isn't *just* a kiss, Quinne. At least it isn't for me."

She blinked and her expression softened slightly, but she didn't say anything.

He worked his jaw, trying to come up with the

words that would help her understand where he was coming from. But instead of saying something eloquent and beautiful, he blurted the first thing that came to his mind. "I refuse to become some distraction you can play with until you get bored."

Her mouth dropped open and a flash of fury clouded her eyes.

Peter let out another groan. "That sounds worse than what I was trying to say." He set his steely gaze on her once more, before taking a breath and releasing it. "I've had love before. I had a wife and a marriage and it slipped through my fingers no matter what I did to try to fix it. If I find love again, I want it to last."

Her eyes darted away and he didn't miss the way her hands balled into fists at her sides. "You don't think I'm capable of being that for you."

The storm that raged within him crashed like waves on the beach. It wasn't that he didn't think she was capable of it. He just didn't trust himself to give his heart to another woman who would inevitably shatter it like it was nothing. Something about the way she'd muttered those words tugged at him like a lure on a fishing line.

Who was he kidding? He'd already been hooked. He'd already given a part of himself, and he hadn't even realized it was happening.

Peter grasped her chin with his finger and thumb, forcing her to look up at him. "I think you are capable of achieving anything you set your mind to. Including loving someone. And you could have any man you want. I just don't know if what I have to offer is what you want. Long term."

Her brows creased and she licked her lips, drawing

his attention to them. She'd said so herself. It was just one kiss. He craved her touch, to feel her lips on his, her hands in his hair.

A curse escaped his lips and he pushed aside all his reservations. His free hand snaked around her waist and he pulled her hard against him, crushing his mouth over hers, claiming her for his own. Quinne gasped, though she didn't pull away. Instead, her hands lifted to clasp around the back of his neck. Her body molded against his, clinging to him like he was breath itself.

Their lips sought each other as they each demonstrated their own desperation. He hadn't realized just how much he had needed this, to feel wanted—desired. A fire exploded within his chest as he allowed himself to succumb to the moment.

Man and woman. Two people with similar wants and needs. He might regret this moment later, but for now he'd let his heart have the win.

Peter nipped at her jawline, trailing kisses along its edge toward her ear. She let out a soft moan, which only spurred him onward. She was like heaven to touch and he wasn't sure he'd have the strength to be the first to pull back... until the front door opened then slammed shut.

"Hey, Dad. I'm home!"

Quinne tore herself from his clutches, turning from him as she placed her palms on the countertop. Her heavy breathing was the only sound he could hear besides the blood rushing in his ears.

"Dad?"

He glanced back at Quinne before raking a hand through his mussed hair. "In the kitchen. Quinne is here," he called. "She's staying for a few days."

Kat's hurried footsteps were followed by her bursting into the kitchen. "Really?" She let out a squeal and rushed past him toward a weakly smiling Quinne. "That's awesome!" Kat stopped suddenly and tilted her head. "What's the matter? Did you get hurt?"

Quinne glanced up at Peter briefly before touching the butterfly bandage on her forehead. "I had a car accident. The doctor thought it would be best if I could stay with someone and I don't really have any family other than my mother. I hope it's okay."

Kat gave Quinne a tight hug. "This is gonna be great! You can sleep in my room if you want."

"I think we'll just let her have the guest room," Peter placed a hand on Kat's shoulder. "Did you get dinner yet?"

She nodded. "We had pizza." Her eyes drifted toward the sushi they'd been making and she wrinkled her nose. "That smells gross. I'm... just gonna go watch some TV."

Peter prayed she didn't hear the strain in his chuckle. "Go for it. Maybe we can do a movie night after Quinne and I eat."

Kat nodded, the smile returning to her face. "Can I pick?"

"Sure."

She shot another look toward Quinne. "There's this really cool movie that just came out on Netflix. You're gonna love it." She darted toward the living room, leaving Peter and Quinne alone once more.

The tension in the air couldn't have been sliced with his sharpest knife.

This was why he hadn't wanted to kiss her.

And yet that one regret was already fading.

Quinne still hadn't said a single thing since she'd pulled away from him. He would have given anything to know what she was thinking. She'd practically pushed him to kiss her. She'd insisted that a kiss wasn't a big deal.

But he knew better. He already wanted more. Peter glanced in the direction Kat had disappeared. At any given moment she could return. Talking to Quinne about what had just happened was dangerous.

Not only would it be dangerous because of Kat—he was terrified that Quinne would brush him off.

Peter scowled. He wasn't going to force her to talk and he didn't want to assume that this meant more than she wanted it to. He'd take his aching heart and the longing he felt, then he'd wrap it up tight and hide it away. He'd gotten over a woman before.

Without a word, he returned to his station and rolled the sushi into shape. As far as he was concerned, nothing had changed. They would go about their evening as they would normally.

He wasn't sure when he noticed, but at some point he could feel Quinne's eyes on him. The hairs on the back of his neck rose and his pulse quickened, returning to a familiar racing pace.

Don't look at her. That will just make things worse.

Peter retrieved a knife and began slicing the sushi. He just had to get through dinner. Then they could have their movie night and he could keep his distance.

Heaven knew that if he got close enough to touch her, the torture of not being able to would end him.

"Peter?" Her quiet voice dragged him from his thoughts. "Are you going to say something?"

Chapter Fifteen

Quinne was still reeling from their kiss. But what infuriated her was how Peter was ignoring her. Her hands balled tightly and she shifted closer to him, her voice dropping to a whisper. "You're the one who made a big deal about what a kiss means."

He flinched, then slowly placed the knife on the counter before turning toward her. "You know very well that we have different views on that topic." His gaze darted toward the door then swung back to meet hers. "And Kat is home. If it's all the same to you, I'd rather keep her out of this."

"Are you *mad*?" She bristled. "*You're* the one who kissed *me*. You're the one who took that step—who crossed over that threshold."

"Don't you think I know that?" His hiss surprised her and she stepped back. He raked another rough hand through his hair. "I messed up. I gave in to something I shouldn't have. The worst part is that I knew better. So maybe you'd take pity on me and just let me lick my wounds."

He picked up the plate of sushi he'd been working on and slid it across the counter toward her. "Eat your dinner."

Peter wiped his hands on a towel then tossed it on the counter before he headed toward the door where his daughter had disappeared. "What about you?"

"What about me?" he muttered.

"Aren't you going to eat?"

He stopped, his back still facing her. "I can't stay in here, Quinne."

A lump formed in her throat as she edged around the island. "Why?"

His shoulders drooped and he hung his head. "Do you really want me to answer that?"

"I wouldn't have asked if I didn't." Though even as she said those words, she wasn't sure. At the moment she felt so off balance. She didn't know what she wanted, except to know where they stood. She didn't dare assume anything.

Peter didn't face her. It was as if they'd both been stuck in a time warp. She couldn't help but hold her breath as she waited for his answer. Finally he turned toward her. A myriad of emotions flitted across his face. Though he didn't move from his spot, she felt as though he had come closer. The room felt smaller somehow.

He shoved his hands into his pockets and lifted his shoulders. "You want the truth?"

"Of course I do," she whispered.

A sigh burst from his lips as he locked his eyes with hers. "I'm not going to stay in here with you because I know if I did, I wouldn't be able to control myself. Being this close to you is... *intoxicating*." His jaw tightened. "And I'm not about to assume that you want the same things that I do."

Chills coursed along her spine, causing a slew of goose bumps. Before she could ask exactly what he meant by wanting the same things, he'd managed to disappear.

Quinne sucked in sharply, her breath shuddering. The kiss they had shared had been unlike anything she had ever experienced. Her whole body had felt like it was on fire. It felt dangerous and exciting, but at the same time she had never felt safer.

What was she doing? She couldn't fall for Peter.

Right?

Most definitely not.

He wasn't the kind of guy she had ever seen herself with. He was too down-to-earth. He had an ex-wife and a kid. His life was messy.

But wasn't hers just as messy? Why *couldn't* they give this—whatever it was—a try?

Her stomach reacted to that thought with a flush of flurries. She pulled her lower lip between her teeth, gnawing on it as she attempted to come up with even one way this could go wrong. But she came up empty.

Okay, there was one thing.

Kat.

Quinne didn't know how Peter's daughter would react. Sure, Kat thought Quinne was fun to spend time with *now*, but would she think Quinne was trying to replace her mother? That was what most of the kids in the movies thought when their parents started dating someone new.

Stomach churning, Quinne shoved the plate of

sushi away from her. All that work for nothing. There was no way she would be able to eat now.

The next two hours were spent seated on a couch with Kat and Peter. The young girl situated herself between the two adults, not a care in the world. Good. She didn't know.

Granted, there wasn't anything to know at this point. Though, the more Quinne thought about it, the more she had to admit to herself that she wasn't entirely against the idea of dating Peter.

He laughed at something on the television and goose bumps returned to Quinne's arms. She glanced over to him only to find his eyes on her. He quickly looked away and she fought the smile that wanted to spread across her face.

If there were zero other variables to worry about, would she want to date him?

Her heart thrummed in the positive.

Peter might not be the kind of guy she would normally have been interested in, but the more she'd gotten to know him the more she realized there were so many things about him that she found attractive.

He was a hard worker and he was a good father. He was protective and serious, but he could make her laugh, too. Anyone would be lucky to have him.

She would be lucky to have him.

And from the looks of it, Peter was interested in her.

A small voice in her head pushed her, nudged her forward. *What do you have to lose? Give it a shot.* It was far more tempting than she wanted to admit.

Even more frightening.

Kat shifted in her seat to get comfortable and eventually snuggled up against her dad. Quinne's heart burst with another bout of adoration. Peter wrapped his arm around his daughter. They were adorable together.

What was holding her back? Sure, she hadn't planned on settling down—with anyone. But being here, in Peter's home with his daughter felt... *right*. She could envision herself here, part of their family.

Suddenly it didn't seem so strange.

The end credits scrolled on the screen and Peter reached for the remote. "Alright, kiddo. Time for bed."

"Aww, but it's only eight. Can't we watch one more?"

He chuckled as he helped Kat to her feet. "One more would put us way past your bedtime."

Kat frowned. "But Quinne is here. She can bring me to Maple Gardens in the morning. So I don't have to go to bed as early."

Peter shot a quick look in Quinne's direction then shook his head before she could agree to such a request. "Quinne has been through a lot today. She needs to get her rest. And her car isn't here."

Kat groaned, but didn't argue further. She turned to Quinne. "Goodnight. I'll see you in the morning."

Quinne offered her a weak smile and a nod then watched her head toward the hallway. Her gaze landed on Peter.

For a moment they didn't say a word to each other. It was as if the weight of their kiss still hung in the air like a magnet. It kept them glued to their places.

Peter was the first to move. He thumbed over his shoulder. "I'm going to make sure she gets into bed. Then I'll show you your room."

She nodded, not trusting her voice.

Something still brewed within her chest. She couldn't just let their conversation end the way it had. She needed to let him know that she was interested. If she didn't say something tonight, she might lose her nerve.

Right now, she was still high on the adrenaline rush of the accident and the moment they'd shared in the kitchen. She could do this. They were both adults, after all.

About ten minutes passed before Peter materialized in front of her. He gestured toward the hallway, indicating she should follow him. Before she could tell him what she was feeling, he slipped away.

Quinne scrambled to her feet and hurried after him. "Peter," she whispered but he didn't seem to hear her. "*Peter.*" This time it was a little louder. He stopped in a doorway and turned around so suddenly she bumped into him. His hands shot out and he grasped her by her upper arms. Her lashes fluttered furiously as she forced herself to meet his questioning gaze.

"Is something wrong?"

She shook her head, hating the fact that she couldn't come up with the coherent words she needed. "You need to explain yourself," she demanded.

His brows lowered and his eyes swirled with a darkness that made her heart flip. "What are you talking about?"

"When you said you wouldn't assume..." She swallowed hard, realizing that he still held her. As much as she wanted to escape, she wanted to get this all out in the open even more. "I think you should make it perfectly clear what you want."

He shook his head this time. "You are in over your

head, Quinne. You forget I've been here before. I know what the risks are. This time I have a great deal more to lose than you do."

"How can you say that?" she snapped. "Are my feelings less important because—I don't know—because I don't have a kid?" Her voice had risen just enough for him to shoot a concerned look down the hallway. In a matter of seconds, he'd spun her around and placed her in the guest room. Then he pushed the door shut, closing them inside with nowhere to escape.

Peter kept his back to her, his hand lingering on the doorknob. "Of course I don't—think that my feelings are more important than yours." His voice was so low she almost didn't hear it. "But you can't deny that if something were to start between us, then I would get the brunt of the aftermath."

Before she could argue with him on that, he faced her.

"If I let you into my life it's not just my heart that could get broken. It's Kat's too."

She stiffened. He was right. Even still, a niggling thought seemed to break through her hesitation. "Do you always base your decisions for happiness on Kat?"

He gave her a sharp look.

Quinne blushed furiously. "What I mean to say is... you're allowed to be happy—even if it is only for a moment. You can't make all of your decisions based on the fear of how they might turn out." She took a deep breath and released it. "Goodness knows if I had done that, I wouldn't have what I do today."

Peter studied her without speaking and she squirmed beneath his stare.

Her eyes dropped to her hands. While she might

have appeared to be calm on the outside, she was a complete mess within. Her heart thudded against her chest as if demanding to be released from its cage. Her lungs wheezed from the ache of holding her breath. She flicked her gaze up to meet his.

"I don't know what you want. But if there is a possibility that we want the same thing, don't you think we ought to give it a chance?" She moved toward him, closing the distance between them. Her pulse roared in her ears and her stomach knotted and tangled in on itself.

Quinne told herself she shouldn't, but she didn't heed her own warning. She reached up and feathered her fingers through the hair at his temple. Her body flushed hot then cold all at once. She'd already released the sails and all she needed was a gust of wind to take her on an adventure.

Without warning, Peter scooped her into his arms. His lips crushed hers.

She pushed her hands into his hair, clinging to him, allowing her heart to take this win. There was no way of telling where the future might go from here, but in this moment she was okay without knowing—without planning.

Being with Peter was like coming home. His arms welcomed her, accepted her. She didn't have to put on a mask for him and for the first time in her life she felt whole.

Chapter Sixteen

Peter shot a look at Quinne as she spoke to the camera on the other side of the Maple Gardens kitchen. She'd been cleared by her doctor last week and he couldn't tell who was more disappointed.

Himself or Kat?

Her eyes flitted over to where he stirred the chili and she smiled before returning her attention to the camera.

Kat stood behind the camera, watching intently and waiting to turn it off when Quinne gave the word. Beside Quinne stood two residents: Alice and Millie. They cracked jokes about the kinds of meals they'd concocted when they were young mothers on a budget.

The kitchen was crowded—something that would have normally irritated him. Today it didn't bother him, and he knew the reason why.

Quinne laughed at something her mother said and her eyes found his. He shook his head, doing his best to keep his chuckle quiet. It was funny how one life change was enough to make his outlook so much better. He'd been a shell of himself since his wife had left him. And now, he'd finally allowed himself to be... happy.

It was more than that, though. Being with Quinne made everything seem easier somehow.

Except when Kat was in the room.

He turned away from Quinne and her work. They'd decided telling Kat would be a bad idea. While she was old enough to understand what dating meant, she might get even more attached than she already was. He didn't want to put either of them in a position where Kat would be brokenhearted if this new relationship didn't pan out. It was best to test the waters first.

"Dad! Wasn't that awesome?"

He jumped when Kat tugged on his arm.

"Quinne is really good when she's being recorded. I wish I could—"

"Absolutely not."

"But—"

He sighed. "I'm not going to discuss this with you right now. You know the rules."

She folded her arms and if she didn't look so serious, her cross expression would have made him laugh. "But there are kids who are a lot younger than me and they have accounts and even their own YouTube channels."

"They're not my kids."

"I wish I wasn't your kid," she mumbled. "I bet Quinne would have let me if she was my mom."

He sent her a sharp look. Where had she gotten that idea from? Had she noticed the way he was treating Quinne lately? She hadn't overheard anything, had she? His flurry of thoughts were quickly squashed. This wasn't about Quinne being her mother. It was about Quinne having different priorities.

Peter faced his daughter and put his hands on both of her shoulders. "You're still young, and right now it's hard for you to understand the way the world works—"

She rolled her eyes.

He worked his jaw and took a deep breath to keep his temper in check. "I need you to trust me. The older you get the more you're going to want to test the waters. You're going to see other kids doing something that you want to do and you're not going to see a problem with it unless someone gets hurt. By then it's too late."

"Dad," she groaned. "I'm old enough to know what's okay and what's dangerous. I get it."

Shaking his head, Peter let out a sigh. "I know you think you do, but you don't. As the adult and your father I see things differently. And that's why I make the rules."

"Your rules suck." She pulled away from him and stomped her foot before charging out of the kitchen.

He glanced over to Quinne, finding her finishing up her conversation with Alice and Millie before escorting them out of the kitchen. When she returned, her expression was tense.

"Is everything okay? Did Kat find out about us?"

Peter chuckled. "No, she didn't find out about us. She's just getting to be that age where she doesn't like certain rules I have put in place. It's perfectly normal." He glanced toward the door, then reached for her hand before lowering his voice. "I just wish we knew how long she was going to be gone, so I knew if I had enough time to kiss you."

Her lips lifted into a smile. “I can’t say I didn’t think the same thing.”

He tugged on her hand, pulling her closer to him but not enough that they couldn’t step back in case someone in particular appeared. “I want to take you on a date—a *real* date.”

Quinne tilted her head slightly. “A date?”

He nodded. “Dinner. Dancing. The whole nine yards.”

She laughed. “That sounds incredibly tempting.”

“I sense a *but* coming.”

Her gaze flitted to the doorway. “What would you tell Kat? She’s bound to notice you’re gone for longer than it takes to get groceries. Have you gone on dates with other women? Is she ready for that kind of change?”

This was one of the reasons he was falling for this woman. She didn’t have any children of her own and yet she was a natural with them. When he’d first met her, he wouldn’t have thought that she had a motherly bone in her body.

She’d proved him wrong time and time again.

Peter lifted her hand to his lips and pressed a kiss to her knuckles. “I haven’t gone on any dates yet. But I don’t think she would mind. Her mother has been open about her dating since our divorce. Kat should be fine.” He offered her a reassuring smile. “Honestly, I feel like she would be more thrilled than anything else. Don’t tell me you forgot the reaction she had when she met you in person.”

Quinne nodded. “Oh, I remember. But I still worry how she’s going to react. You’re her father. And dating is one thing, but dating *me*—”

"Would be a dream come true."

She pursed her lips to the side. "Do you mind if I spent some special time with her one-on-one before you tell her we're going out?"

"I wasn't planning on telling her it was you. I was just going to explain that I wanted to see other women."

She tugged her hand from his with a gasp. "Other *women*, huh? What aren't you telling me?"

He snatched her hand back, this time forcing her body to collide with his. Voice lowering, he murmured into her ear, "You are the only woman I am interested in spending my time with, and don't you forget it." His other arm slipped around her waist, securing her in her place. "You are the only one who fills my thoughts, makes my heart soar, and makes me remember the man I wanted to be. I don't plan on that changing any time soon."

Quinne let out a shaky breath. "Noted," she whispered.

"What are you guys doing?"

Peter's head snapped in the direction of the door, finding Kat standing there with her hands on her hips. She looked utterly confused.

Quinne gasped and stepped back. What a way to *not* make it obvious.

They'd been caught. There was no way around it. Kat surely could put two and two together. Peter rubbed the back of his neck, wondering if he should grab Quinne's hand and bring her forward as if offering a sacrifice.

But Quinne beat him to it.

The woman he was falling for smiled widely as she

stepped toward Kat. "I was thinking about doing a segment on dancing. Your dad was a willing subject and I was teaching him how to properly hold a lady."

Kat's eyes darted toward her father. "Really?" She didn't sound like she believed Quinne in the least. "Dad doesn't dance."

"That's why I wanted to teach him. I was thinking we could do a segment here at Maple Gardens where we teach the residents how to dance and your father graciously agreed."

Wait, what?

His eyes shot to hers and his mouth fell open, but then he remembered he needed to sell this. How was Quinne able to lie so easily? It was as if she'd been trained to do it.

Kat's brows lifted and she laughed. "You think I'm gonna believe that? My dad doesn't dance and he definitely doesn't do social media."

"It's true, Kat." He was backed into a corner. There was nowhere to escape. Either he needed to come clean or he needed to allow Quinne to take the lead on this one. Funny, that was the guy's job in dancing and now he'd just agreed to be her guinea pig in her little channel.

Kat gaped at him. "But you said—"

"I said you were too young to be on the show. I'm not a ten-year-old, now am I?"

She pouted, before glancing at Quinne. "Can I go to Tiffany's house? Quinne's done with her video, and this is getting boring."

Peter nodded. "Do you need a ride?"

She shook her head. "I'll see if her mom can get me." She held out her hand. "Can I use your phone?"

"Is your homework done?"

She let out an exaggerated groan, leading him to believe she thought that was a stupid question.

Before he gave her the device, he glanced over to Quinne once more. "I wanted to talk to you about something. I know you're a little frustrated about things right now—"

"I'm fine," she muttered.

"Okay, but I wanted to ask you what you thought about me dating."

Kat's expression shifted to something unreadable. She just stared at him like she'd turned to stone.

"I wanted to ask you before I started taking anyone out, because I didn't want you to be uncomfortable."

His daughter shrugged then looked away. "I don't care. Mom's dating someone. You should be able to. Now, can I call Tiffany?"

Peter gave her the phone. "Make sure you check with her mom on how long you can stay."

Kat took the phone without another word and exited the kitchen.

Without her presence the room almost felt colder. Peter met Quinne's eyes and laughed. "Well, there you have it. She's okay with me dating. And she doesn't know a thing."

Quinne leaned against the counter where she stood. She had her arms crossed over her chest and she let out a bark of laughter. "Oh, she definitely knows."

"Knows what?"

"That we're the ones you were referring to when you brought up dating. Seriously, haven't you ever heard of being subtle? Do you even know the meaning of flying under the radar?"

He stiffened, glancing toward the door. “But she didn’t say anything. She—”

Another sharp laugh. “Dude, you have to be blinkered not to see what you just did. She caught us together in a compromising position.”

“But you covered it up—which, by the way, you totally owe me for.”

She wagged a finger at him. “Nope. This is all on you. I might have covered it up with a flimsy excuse, but you had to go and tear that whole thing down the second you brought up dating. There is only one woman she has probably seen you with—”

“Excuse me? Did you seriously say *probably*?”

A smile tugged at her lips. “As I was saying, she’s ten. She’s not an idiot. She could have put it all together with her eyes closed.”

“Nah. She’s also a kid and she would have said something if she thought we were getting close.”

Quinne shook her head. “I’m telling you. This isn’t what you think it is.”

“Whether it is or it isn’t, we’ve got the green light and I’m going to take you out on Friday night.

“Fine.”

“Good.”

She laughed. “This is why I love you.”

He stiffened at the very moment she did. Her face flushed hot and her eyes grew wide.

“I didn’t mean—”

“I love you, too.” The words slipped out before he could wrangle them in. But, surprisingly, they were exactly how he felt.

Chapter Seventeen

Quinne couldn't believe this was happening. She wasn't ready for a relationship. How could she say she was in love? It was all too soon, right?

Or maybe it wasn't.

So much was right about this new relationship. Peter was a terrific father. Kat was an awesome kid. Both of them treated her as if she belonged with them and she certainly felt the same. But love was a big step and one which could lead to heartbreak. It mattered to Quinne that Kat saw her as a friend and someone she could rely upon.

She was a mature adult. There was no reason she couldn't start seeing someone who had a kid. Besides, Kat wasn't really a kid in the traditional sense. Over the years Quinne had met her share of child influencers and some of them were as young as six. Kat was inching ever closer to being a teenager and it was showing. That was one of the big reasons why Quinne wanted to get closer to Kat in a way that would help her relationship with the girl's father continue to improve.

But the last two days, Kat had seemed distant. She did her homework without chatting as much and when it came time to work on Quinne's videos, she did everything she was asked without asking a million questions.

They sat at a table in the main hall while Kat worked on her multiplication. She fiddled with her pencil rather than writing down the answers.

"You need some help?" Quinne leaned closer to see the problem.

Kat shook her head.

"You've been stuck on that problem for longer than usual. Are you sure you don't want a hint?"

The girl glanced at her, eyes delving into her like she was far wiser than her years. "Do you like my dad?"

Quinne let out a strangled chuckle. "Of course I like him." This was it. The moment she'd been waiting for. Hadn't she told Peter this would happen? And now it was happening to her rather than Peter.

"No. I mean *like* him like him."

There was no getting out of this. Quinne had seen that from the second Kat set her gaze on her in the beginning. The first fib was so much easier. This felt like Quinne was dangling off a life raft and her answer would dictate whether or not she'd be saved.

Just great.

"I guess if you don't want to tell me..."

Quinne reached forward and touched Kat's forearm. "I want you to trust me. And if this is the conversation you feel ready to have, then I'll answer anything you ask me honestly."

"Did you kiss?"

She gaped at the girl. It was like a switch had gone

off in her brain, not allowing any of the electrical neurons and synapses to do their job. "What?"

"Kiss. Did you guys kiss?"

Quinne didn't know why her gaze flitted to where Peter would appear if he were to come check on them. Perhaps she was hoping he would rescue her from this sinking ship on his own. All she knew was that he hadn't wanted to tell Kat yet. Would she be breaking his trust by ringing that bell?

"If you did, I won't be mad." Kat looked away, lifting a shoulder. Her voice was soft but unreadable. "My mom dates different guys all the time." Her eyes darted up to meet Quinne's again. "My dad hasn't dated anyone since they got divorced. I was just wondering..." Her voice trailed off and once again she broke eye contact. She seemed to sit quietly in her thoughts for a little while then she sighed. "I just don't think it's a good idea for him to date someone if they don't like him back."

Quinne stiffened. Man, this girl was wise beyond her years. Had she really noticed how different her parents were? Chewing on the inside of her cheek, Quinne contemplated what she could say that would be truthful but also give this girl some peace of mind. The relationship Quinne had with Peter was still new. It was in that beginning stage where anything seemed possible. But she knew better than to believe there was a guarantee it would go the distance.

There was no telling how far they would take things. They could break up in a week. Or they could get married.

That latter thought started a strange feeling inside

her, warm tingles danced along her insides. She didn't realize she was even smiling until Kat spoke up again.

"You said you would answer honestly."

Quinne pressed her lips together tightly and nodded. "You're right. I did." She took a deep breath then let it out slowly, but that didn't help quell her nerves. "I *do* really like your dad." She had to bite back a smile when she continued. "And we have kissed."

Kat didn't react right away. Her gaze seemed to drill into Quinne's soul as she studied her for what felt like an eternity. "Are you going to leave him when you get bored?"

Her head reared back. "Am I—*what*? Where did you get an idea like that?"

The young girl shrugged again. "My mom finds someone new when she gets bored. I hear her talking about it on the phone."

Quinne glanced toward the kitchen. She couldn't imagine Peter being thrilled about his daughter having this kind of view regarding relationships. Quinne shook her head, scooting to the edge of her seat. "I don't know the future, so I can't promise anything. But I can tell you that I'm not the type of person who walks away from something—or someone—because I'm bored."

Bother. That probably sounded like she was putting down Kat's mother. She watched Kat carefully, hoping she would be able to tell the way the girl was feeling. This had to be the strangest conversation they'd had since they met, and Quinne only had herself to blame. If she hadn't allowed herself to get close to Peter, then she wouldn't be in this predicament.

Suddenly Kat's expression shifted into something

more relaxed. She smiled before nodding and turning back to her work. "Okay."

"Okay?"

Another nod. "He likes you too."

Quinne snorted. "What?"

"I can tell. He *really* likes you."

Goose bumps trailed up and down Quinne's arms. "Yeah?"

"Yep. I think he might even love you."

Her mouth went dry. They'd only said those words once to each other and it had almost felt like they didn't count due to the circumstances surrounding the conversation. The funny thing was that she didn't mind Kat making that comment. Quinne swallowed at the lump that had formed in the back of her throat. "How can you tell?"

Kat glanced at her briefly before she scribbled an answer on her paper. "Because he let you come to our house. No one gets to do that."

"That doesn't mean anything. You said your dad hasn't dated anyone since he split up with your mom." Quinne snapped her mouth shut. She was heading down a dangerous path right now. Shouldn't she be keeping things more professional between herself and this girl? Kat was hardly old enough to be considered one of Quinne's girlfriends, who she could hash things out with. "Never mind. Forget I said anything."

Kat peered at her with what could only be described as curiosity. "Do you think he doesn't love you?"

Quinne laughed if only to prevent herself from saying something she might regret. "I don't know." How could she tell Kat that he'd admitted his feelings to her already? She couldn't. Especially if Peter hadn't had that talk with his daughter yet.

"You don't know?" Kat tilted her head slightly. "Aren't you supposed to love each other before you kiss?"

Oh, the innocence of youth.

Quinne laughed again. "I suppose you make a good point." This conversation had gone off the rails. A lot of this should probably have been discussed with her father. Quinne was overstepping.

Then again, maybe not.

Quinne was a role model for millions of girls on her social media platforms. Why couldn't she be the same thing for Kat, but in person? The word stepmother came to mind, as if against her will. Boy, that word left a strange taste in her mouth. But that didn't mean she couldn't be a good one, did it?

She didn't know how long she got lost in thought, but when Kat flipped her book shut and got to her feet, she was dragged back to the present. "You're done already?"

Kat gave her a strange look. "Yeah. That's why I closed my book." She glanced around the area where they'd been working. "You wanna go exploring or something? Dad doesn't get off work for a few hours and I don't feel like being cooped up in here."

Quinne's focus shifted toward the kitchen. Peter would probably tell her to go for it—especially if they stayed on the grounds. This might be the best opportunity she had to get to know Kat on a deeper level. Something told her that if she did, then the relationship she had with Peter would only grow stronger.

She clapped her hands together and nodded. "Sure. That sounds like fun. Let's go exploring."

The only way to describe Kat's expression was utter joy. "Really?"

"Yeah, why not?"

"I dunno. I just thought you would probably tell me that I should get more work done or do something *productive*." She made a face with that last word.

Quinne chuckled. "Look at who you're talking to. I'm Quinne Hart. I don't follow the rules all of the time."

Kat's smile widened, even though it didn't seem possible. "I guess you are. Where do you want to explore?"

"You're the leader on this little trip. Where do you want to go?"

"There's a pond out behind the community with ducks. Do you think we could go feed them some bread or something?"

Quinne grimaced. "Actually, feeding wild ducks bread is not great. They need something similar to what they would forage for themselves."

Kat frowned, her whole body seeming to go a little more limp than before. "Oh."

"But if you wanted to see if your dad has some frozen peas or oats, those would be better for our little feathered friends."

Without a word, Kat darted for the kitchen, causing Quinne to have to compensate for her head start. She jogged after Kat, reaching the kitchen just as Kat was removing a large bag from the freezer. "We need these," she explained as if that statement was all Peter would require as an explanation.

"Wait, what?" His eyes darted toward Quinne, lingering a little longer than she was expecting. But then she blinked and the spell was broken. "Is someone hurt?"

"What?" Kat laughed as she headed toward Quinne. "Why would I want peas if someone was hurt? It's not like they have any healing properties or anything."

"No, you use them for—" He shook his head. "Never mind. Just—what do you need them for? You've neglected to tell me that little tidbit of information."

"We're gonna feed the ducks."

Once again, Peter glanced at Quinne, bewildered. "Peas?"

Quinne shrugged. "I told her we couldn't feed them with bread. We needed something else."

"*Peas.*"

She bit back a smile, loving the tone of his voice almost more than the look on his face. "Yup. We'll be back by the time you clock out."

He took a step toward her, snaking an arm around her waist and she gasped. Quinne's eyes sought Kat, but found she'd slipped from the room at some point. Quinne shook her head, laughing as she did so. "You can't take me off guard like that."

Peter's voice lowered to that husky tone she loved so much. "Yeah? Why not?"

"Because," she shoved his chest with her fingertips, "Kat could have seen us."

He looked over her shoulder toward the door. "But she didn't. And I have a feeling she's already halfway to that creek by now, so you might as well kiss me."

"I might as well, huh?"

His gaze danced as he tucked a strand of hair

behind her ear. "Yeah," he whispered. "I've missed you."

"We literally see each other every day."

"Not like this."

She cocked her head to the side, a smile stealing across her face. "Perhaps that could change if you were to tell your daughter about your intentions."

His expression faltered. Did she catch a hint of fear in those gorgeous eyes of his? Was he actually worried about taking that next step?

She didn't know how she felt about that. On the one hand, she didn't want to move too fast and end up getting hurt because of it. But on the other, she wanted to see where things were headed. The uncertainty of the future continued to lurk in the back of her mind, ever since they'd shared that first kiss.

Quinne forced aside those thoughts, shaking her head to clear it. She pulled away from him, letting her fingers glide down his arm and grasp his hand briefly before she released him. "I'll see you in a few hours. I should probably go make sure your daughter doesn't do something ridiculous."

He nodded, turning back to what he was working on. "Love you."

Her back was to him and she froze in the doorway. She could pretend she hadn't heard him.

She should definitely pretend she hadn't heard that.

This was the second time he'd told her he loved her, and she couldn't bring herself to say it back. The only time she'd said she loved him was flippant at best. She still wasn't sure she was ready to give her whole heart to him like that.

Chapter Eighteen

Peter muttered a strong word under his breath. He couldn't believe he'd just admitted his feelings to Quinne *again* and in such a stupid manner. They hadn't talked about their feelings again since that one time. That conversation still hovered over his head demanding to be dealt with. Maybe it was time to finally have that talk.

He didn't dare turn around to see if she had heard him.

Who was he kidding? There was no way she *hadn't* heard him. This kitchen echoed like nobody's business. Now there was no doubt that Quinne knew how he felt, which only made her lack of reciprocation that much worse.

Peter let out another curse and tossed the knife he'd been using onto the counter. Metal clanged then scraped against the surface before it came to a stop a little way from the edge.

He hunched over, grasping the edge of the counter with both of his hands. This confession would be the thing that pushed him over the edge. He had to take her out and talk about it, otherwise he'd drive himself crazy.

The only problem was that he couldn't be sure what she would say to him. The last time he'd brought this up, she'd wanted to make Kat more comfortable with her—or something along those lines.

Ironically, he couldn't think of a single person who his daughter was *more* comfortable with than Quinne. Well, except himself and her mother.

Peter couldn't envision anything bad happening with Kat finding out about them.

Was it possible they were each making excuses because they didn't want to take that next step?

His jaw tightened and he spun around to lean against the metal countertop. Well, the time for putting it off had finally come to an end. He wasn't going to take no for an answer. And to solidify everything, he'd be having a very important discussion with Kat.

"We need to talk."

His daughter glanced over at him on their car ride home. "Okay."

"I know we haven't discussed me getting back out in the world and dating, but—"

"You want to date Quinne."

He clamped his mouth shut. Apparently he wasn't as good at hiding his intentions as he thought he was.

"It's fine, Dad. I've known for a little while already."

"And you're not upset?"

"I'm not *not* upset."

"What does that even mean?" He let out a sigh. "I can't do cryptic with you tonight, Kat. I wanted to have this discussion to bring everything to the front. I want us to be able to tell each other everything."

"Do you love her?"

Wow. "That came out of left field."

She shrugged.

"Is there a reason you're asking me that?"

Kat eyed him. "I want to know if you love her because you told me that people who are in love kiss each other. And Quinne said you kissed."

His eyes widened. "She told you that?"

"I asked her."

"Why would you ask her something like that?" He could hear the edge creep into his voice and he had to work a little harder at keeping it level.

"Are you mad?"

"Mad?" He let out a dry chuckle. "You just caught me off guard."

"Well, do you love her?"

Peter glanced at her, then back at the road as they continued their drive home. "Yes, I think I do."

She smiled, though it wasn't as genuine as some of the others she'd shared. "Good."

"Would my dating her make you feel uncomfortable?"

"No." Kat responded so matter-of-factly that her statement threw him for a loop again.

"You're not?"

"Not if you love her. It's... weird... knowing you care about her."

He shot a look at her out of the corner of his eye. "Why is that?"

"Because I liked her first."

Peter didn't even know how to respond to her statement. She had a point. When he'd first met Quinne, he had thought the worst of her. Now, he couldn't get her out of his thoughts. "I guess that goes to show that you have excellent taste when it comes to first impressions." He was relieved to find her expression softened at his compliment.

"Yeah, I do." She faced him more fully. "If you love her, and you kiss her, does that mean you want to marry her?"

"*What*?"

"You know, like with you and Mom. Do you want to get married?"

Peter had to take a calming breath after his coughing fit. When he could finally speak, he met her gaze. "I don't have an answer to that one. Not yet."

"How come?"

"Because things like that take time to figure out."

The creases in her forehead deepened. "But you love her—"

"When you started learning your multiplication, did you know them all right off the bat?"

"No."

"No," he repeated. "But you built on what you learned little by little. I'm doing that with Quinne. I'm learning what I love about her a little bit every day. And when I think I've learned enough to make that decision, you'll be the first one I tell."

That one earned him a smile that was brighter than any star in the sky. "Okay," she said firmly. "Deal."

"Hey, Dad, Olivia said I could use some of the office supplies she has in the back for a project I'm working on. Can I go look?"

Out of habit, Peter glanced at Quinne when he answered. "Sure, honey. How long will you be?"

"I dunno. If you need me, Olivia can tell you where I'm at." She faced Quinne. "Wanna come?"

Quinne's eyes locked with Peter's and she shook her head, a smile touching her lips. "I can't, sweetie. I have a few more things I need to prep for tomorrow's video. But if you end up needing any help, you come get me, okay?"

"Okay." Kat bounced out of the room, leaving Peter alone with Quinne for the first time since he'd admitted he loved her. The worst part was that he knew she'd heard him, but she'd intentionally ignored it. That could mean so many things, the worst one being that she hadn't gotten to the same level of affection as he had.

The quiet in the room was heavier than usual. Their unspoken conversation weighed on him, making it harder to breathe. There was no telling how long Kat would be gone and he didn't want to have this conversation in front of an audience.

Peter watched Quinne as she skimmed through something on her tablet. The fact she hadn't left the room to avoid him was a good sign, surely?

"You can stop staring at me like that." Quinne swiped her finger across the screen again without looking up. "You might as well say what you're going to say." This time she glanced up at him. She wasn't smiling, but she didn't seem upset either. She placed the tablet on the counter then rested her elbows there. She looked so nonchalant about the whole thing, which only made him feel even more self-conscious.

"Okay."

She lifted a brow. "Okay," she said flatly. "At this rate the sun is going to set before you get out what you really want to say."

"Hey," he scoffed. "This is harder than you think. May I remind you that I've said those words twice and you've only said them once."

Her lips twitched. "You know, I had a lot to think about last night. When you said... what you said yesterday, my gut reaction was that I wasn't ready."

He stiffened. So, there it was. Quinne said so herself. She wasn't prepared to move to the next level, at least not yet. He'd have to be patient. He could do that.

"The thing is that I haven't had...well, I've always buried myself in work rather than relationships." Her skin flushed and she straightened from where she stood, then tapped the screen of her tablet absently. "When you told me you loved me, it sorta became real."

"And that's a bad thing?"

"No. Of course not. I'm just..." she blew out a heavy breath. "This is stupid. I'm totally overthinking this."

"What are you overthinking?" He needed to tread carefully. She was clearly hesitant to open her heart to him for whatever reason.

"I don't know. I guess I like to think ahead, and we have Kat to consider. What if..." She sighed again. "What if I'm not mother material?"

He blinked. That wasn't where he had thought she'd go with this. His knee-jerk reaction was to tell her she was being ridiculous. He'd seen the way she was with Kat. She had to know that being a good role model wasn't about being related by blood. It took patience and caring, both qualities that she possessed. But the words wouldn't come. Anything he might say would sound like he was just trying to manipulate her.

The coloring of her skin deepened and she let out a strained laugh. "I must sound crazy, right? We're not to that point yet."

He surged forward until he stood beside her. Taking her hand in his, he shook his head. "First of all, I think you need to take a good long look at how well you get along with Kat. She loves spending time with you."

Quinne gave him a disbelieving look. "We both know that doesn't mean I would be a good mother figure."

"It's a start."

She gnawed on her lower lip. "Does that mean you think this relationship could get to that point?"

He hesitated, not because he didn't know the answer to that question, but because he did and he wasn't sure she was ready to hear it.

Her eyes flew wide and she pulled her hand from his. "Oh my gosh. I can't believe I'm even suggesting—asking that kind of question."

Peter snatched her hand again, reeling her back toward him. "Yes."

Quinne blinked. "Yes?"

He studied her face, tucking her hair behind her ear. She couldn't be more perfect for him, and the funny thing was that it didn't take long at all for him to come to that realization. "Yes, I could see our relationship heading down that road." The back of Peter's hand traced down her jawline. "I'm all in."

"You are?" she murmured breathily.

"One hundred and ten percent." Peter grasped her chin with his finger and thumb, tilting her face so he got a clear view of her eyes. "The only thing we need to figure out is where you stand in all of this. What do you want, Quinne?" He moved closer, his voice lowering. "Just tell me what you want."

A shuddering breath escaped her lips. Her eyes dipped to his mouth then bounced back to his eyes. "I want you," she whispered. "I want us." She took a deep breath, then let it out slowly through pursed lips. "I think I'm falling in love with you, Peter."

The corners of his mouth quirked upward. "Good. Because I love you, too." His hand grasped her hip and he pulled her body against his. Peter captured her lips, claiming her with a kiss that stole the breath from his lungs. She had managed to make him realize just how dull his life had been before he'd met her, and he didn't want to risk losing this new feeling.

Quinne's arms wrapped around him as she clung to him. Her body melted against his and he lost his bearings as they deepened their kiss. He relinquished himself to her, giving her everything he had. Even if he wanted to, he knew he wouldn't be able to hold anything back. Their once gentle and hesitant kiss shifted into something more demanding. She clutched his shirt in her fists, pulling on it as if he was the only thing that kept her from drowning.

That's when he realized: he'd do anything for her.

Someone cleared their throat and Quinne broke away from him, her hand covering her mouth. He spun around to find Olivia standing in the doorway, her brow lifted and a smile spread wide across her face.

"You're kinda lucky I was the one who walked in on you two. My suggestion? Save it until you get home." She held up a folder. "Here's the new budget for next month. Let me know if you need anything changed." Olivia dropped the folder onto the closest counter. "Oh, and by the way. I think you guys are totally cute together. I guess Alice knew what she was doing when she set you up."

Quinne stepped forward. "Wait, what? My mom didn't set us up."

Olivia shrugged, laughing as she left again. "She won't see it that way."

Quinne faced Peter, touching her lips again. "Well, I guess that's that then."

He moved toward her. "Yeah. I guess so." Peter shot his eyes toward the door then back to her. "I have to say, Olivia had a point—about us remaining professional while we're here. Don't want another interruption like that." His gaze swept over her face, lingering on her lips before meeting her eyes. "But I get the feeling it's going to be a lot harder than I want to admit."

She chuckled, taking a step backward. "I guess it's a good thing Kat will be around. She makes a pretty good chaperone."

Peter lunged forward, capturing her in his arms. "One more," he murmured against her lips. "For the road."

Quinne smiled against his kiss before she pulled away. "Okay, now get back to work."

Chapter Nineteen

The next several weeks were unbearable—but not for the reasons Quinne had expected. When Peter mentioned that it would be hard to keep his hands to himself, she hadn't realized just how right he was.

Every few minutes her thoughts would wander to him and how it felt to be so consumed by him that she felt she could burst into flames. The heat from his touch was enough to ignite her entire being.

She had never felt like this with anyone—to feel this alive was more than thrilling, it was enlightening. Every thought, every action was done with Peter in mind.

Thankfully Kat was just as on board with this whole relationship thing. Quinne found it so much easier to get close to her after the news was out in the open. Things couldn't be going more smoothly.

Well, maybe that was an overstatement. Occasionally, Kat would have her moods. Those moments were few and far between, but it made Quinne question her abilities even after Peter had assured her that no one was perfect. On one such occasion, Kat's friend Tiffany came over to the house to hang out. Tiffany was glued to her phone. She picked it up with every notification, then wouldn't put it down for several minutes afterward.

Quinne sat at the kitchen table, observing the two girls in the living room. Eventually Kat sighed. "Do you have to keep looking at your phone?"

Tiffany glanced at her friend. "I mean, I don't *have* to. But there's some really cool videos right now."

Kat moved closer. "There is?"

Tiffany put her phone down. "It's not a big deal. I know your dad doesn't like you watching stuff."

Kat frowned. "My dad doesn't let me do anything cool."

"Why won't he let you get a phone yet? You're old enough."

Kat glanced toward Quinne then back to her friend. She shrugged. "I don't know. He just says that there's a lot of stuff that isn't good for us."

Tiffany's forehead wrinkled. "He knows he can control what you see, right? That's what my mom and dad did. They let me get an account, but I had to give them my password and they get to see what I post."

Kat sighed, turning her attention to the movie they had running. "I don't think my dad would ever do something like that."

"It's 'cos he's not very cool." Tiffany seemed to make it look like she wasn't gesturing toward Quinne but it was hard to miss. "I bet she would let you get an account."

Quinne stiffened. She shot a quick look at the clock on the wall. Peter wouldn't be home for another hour and she wasn't sure if she wanted to be brought into this conversation. Peter had made it clear he didn't want Kat to be in front of the camera and he limited Kat's screen time. She'd never considered how complicated parenting might be when it came to balancing that kind of thing. But although Kat complained about Peter's rules, at least she kept to them.

She returned her focus to the magazine she had open on the table. This wasn't her decision to make. If the girls asked for her help, she needed to make them wait for Peter.

Quinne could feel Kat's eyes on her without even looking up. Surely it wouldn't be so bad if Kat had the same freedoms as her friends. She glanced over to Kat, and sure enough, found both girls staring at her. She let out an exaggerated sigh. "What do you guys need?"

"We thought maybe you would set up a TikTok account on your phone for Kat" Tiffany sat up on the cushion, looking over the back of the couch. "Don't you think it would be good for her to see what's out there right now?"

Kat didn't say anything—probably because she knew what her father would say.

Even still, Quinne hesitated. Hadn't she wanted to get closer to Kat in any way she could? This might be one of those ways. She'd seen Peter let Kat use his phone for stuff like this. How else had she become familiar with Quinne's content? Would it really be so different if she let Kat set up an account on a device that wasn't her own?"

Quinne peered at Kat. "I'm pretty sure your dad wouldn't agree.'

Kat's face reddened and she jumped up from the

couch. “I use his phone *all* the time. I bet he’d say it was okay for me to use yours. Please, Quinne. Please.”

This was a bonding moment. She wasn’t going to get closer to Kat if she didn’t at least try to reach her through a means on which they could relate but she had no intention of breaking Peter’s rule. Kat’s expression was so hopeful that Quinne almost caved. Instead, she compromised. ‘I won’t set up an account for you, Kat but I do have more than one myself. One of them has nothing on it. No likes or follows or videos so I guess you could use that for a bit.’

The girls exchanged excited glances then hopped off the couch and hurried over to the table. Those fleeting moments of being unsure disappeared. It was nice to be the cool kid again.

Their three heads were still huddled over Quinne’s phone when the front door swung open. “Guess who picked up Chinese?” Peter called.

Quinne glanced up first and a grin stole across her face. She offered Kat her phone then hurried toward the man she loved, throwing her arms around his neck and kissing him deeply.

He slipped his arm around her waist, still holding the plastic bag that contained the food he’d brought. “Mmm,” he murmured against her lips. “I’m not usually a fan of getting dessert first, but I’ll take it.”

“Ew. Gross,” Tiffany called.

Quinne pulled away, biting down on her lower lip to keep the smile at bay, but was incredibly unsuccessful. She glanced up at Peter from beneath her lashes. “We should probably...”

He didn’t release her. “Let them watch. I’m allowed to kiss the woman I love.”

Both girls groaned this time. "Get a room," Kat called out, to which her friend laughed.

"They're in a good mood." He headed for the kitchen island and put the food down. "But it looks like they've grown bored with you already."

Quinne snickered. "Not quite. I let Kat use a TikTok account on my phone which is empty—"

He stilled, the hand holding a white carton freezing mid-air as he stared at her. "You did what?"

She blinked, glancing toward the girls to see if they felt the sudden shift in the air. Neither one of them seemed to notice, so she moved closer to Peter and lowered her voice. "It's fine. She's using my phone so it's not like she's being tracked or anything."

He put the food down and closed his eyes as he took a deep breath and exhaled. "I thought I made it clear I didn't want her on those platforms."

"She doesn't have her own account."

He shot her a dark look.

Quinne shifted uncomfortably. "She can't access it except on my phone." She was scrambling to make sense of why he appeared so upset.

Peter didn't move. He looked like he'd been turned to stone. He wasn't glaring at her, but the mask he wore was just as daunting. "I can't believe you went against my wishes and—"

"You said you didn't want her in front of the camera —" she stammered. "And she's clearly seen my videos. She said she watches them on your phone."

"That's not the point, Quinne!" he muttered sharply. His eyes darted over to the girls, then he strode toward Quinne and led her by her upper arm to the other side of the room. "The point is that I'm trying to keep her away from that stuff for as long as possible. There are so many dangers for a girl her age." He pinched the bridge of his nose. "I can't believe I thought you'd understand—"

"Hey, that's not really fair." Her defenses rose, causing her chest to tighten and cut off the oxygen to her lungs. "I listened to you. What's the harm—" She cut herself off and shook her head. He wasn't going to see things her way. And he was right about one thing. He was Kat's father. He had the final say when it came to stuff like this. "You're right. I'm sorry."

Peter opened his mouth then snapped it shut.

"I'll go log her out and I won't let her use my phone again." She moved toward the girls, feeling like she'd been kicked in the stomach. She'd thought she was doing the right thing in getting closer to Kat. But she'd made a grave mistake. Apparently there was a line between being Kat's friend and being someone she could look up to.

He stopped her before she even got a few inches away. The anger had dissipated somewhat, leaving him looking more irritated than anything else. "You can let her use it while Tiffany is here. Then once she's gone, log Kat out."

Quinne nodded. "Okay," she whispered.

His finger hooked under her chin and he studied her a little closer. He didn't apologize for getting upset. But then again, why would he? Kat was his daughter, and he was already dealing with a lot right now. Just the other day she'd overheard him talking with his lawyer about the current custody battle going on. It appeared Kat's mother wasn't going to let go of her rights as easily as Peter had thought.

Quinne pulled away from him, her stomach roiling with the guilt and shame she felt over being conned by the girls into thinking this was okay. Hindsight was definitely twenty-twenty. "I'm going to use the bathroom. I'll be right back."

He didn't release her immediately either—just continued to stare at her like he was trying to figure out a way to tell her she was an idiot without making a scene.

She slipped from his grasp, rubbing her arm where he'd held her. It didn't hurt, but the sudden change in temperature had made it tingle and not in the way she liked. Whether Quinne liked it or not, she was in a relationship with a man who had a near-teenage daughter.

And teens were notorious for finding loopholes. It shouldn't have surprised her that Kat and Tiffany had played on Quinne's desire to be the fun one.

But it did. Even more so, it hurt realizing that Kat didn't seem to care how this decision would affect her relationship with Peter. There was no way he'd trust her as fully as he had before he got home. In fact, there was a strong possibility he'd want to supervise their interactions more regularly.

It was like she'd thought.

She wasn't mother material.

Quinne spent the rest of the evening aloof. Starting with dinner and through the movie they ended up watching. Peter's demeanor had shifted back to his usual easy-going self. He slipped his arm around her shoulders like he always did, but something felt off. She couldn't bring herself to cuddle into the crook of his arm anymore.

About halfway through the movie, she shot to her feet. "I think I'm going to head out."

"But you don't have a car."

"I'll get an Uber." Her gaze bounced from Peter to Kat and Tiffany. "I'm not feeling so great. I think I just need to turn in early. I'll see you tomorrow, okay?"

Peter got to his feet. "I'll walk you out—"

She forced a smile as she shook her head. "Don't worry about it. I'll be fine."

"You sure?" His brows pulled together and he stepped toward her.

Holding up both hands, she nodded. "Of course. Just enjoy the rest of the movie." She prayed he'd listen to her so she could go home and lick her wounds in peace.

It felt like an eternity before Peter nodded and slowly returned to his seat. "I'll see you tomorrow."

Not even the fresh air outside could soothe the ache she felt. The only way to fix this was to let some time pass. That's how most embarrassing moments were dealt with. She'd be fine, she'd just try to forget this whole night and how it had made her feel like the most incompetent woman on the planet.

Chapter Twenty

Quinne was distant over the next two weeks and spent less time at Peter's place, which made him wonder if he'd overreacted. But every time he went over what had happened, he couldn't find a single thing he'd done wrong.

He hadn't yelled at her. And after their argument, everything seemed to have improved. She'd apologized and that was that.

While he set to work prepping the food for the day, his thoughts continued to bounce around his head. Maybe he was just tired. He'd been working hard at Maple Gardens, fighting for the custody of his daughter, and trying to grow a relationship when he hadn't had one in years.

It was all too much. At some point something had to give.

Right now he just had to be grateful that there was a light at the end of the tunnel in one thing. While Rachel was still fighting him about the custody agreement for Kat, the lawyer said she wasn't going to get everything she wanted unless something changed drastically. They finally had a court date, which would mean Rachel would be arriving in Georgia soon, or she'd forfeit all of her rights.

Thankfully, Kat wasn't aware of any of this and she didn't have to deal with her mother's irresponsibility. But that did present one big problem. He didn't know how he was going to tell his daughter that her mother would be in town but wouldn't be visiting. It felt like Kat was finally coming to accept her life here.

He let out a sigh as he shut the fridge door and leaned against it. A lot of that was probably due to a specific individual who had managed to keep Kat's mind off the fact that she wasn't supposed to spend the last few months at a retirement facility with her father.

Peter glanced around the kitchen, seeing evidence of both his daughter and the woman he loved lying around.

They'd opted to get supplies to feed the ducks again, and he couldn't help but wonder if Quinne was the one making that decision. They probably should have another talk. Maybe he could make it sound less like he was upset with Quinne and emphasize the worries he had over his child accessing stuff online.

From the custody stuff to the relationship, he felt like he was dangling off a cliff, holding on to a rock that had grown increasingly unstable. He could feel his grip loosening and he didn't know what to do about it.

He slipped down the front of the refrigerator and sat on the floor, his head bumped against the cold stainless-steel finish and he closed his eyes. Things always got worse before they got better, right? This could be that moment.

Then his custody battle would work out with Kat, and Quinne would come around. And everything would be the way it was supposed to be.

A buzzing in his pocket drew his attention. He sighed and reached for his phone. The caller ID made his head pound more. Peter pinched the bridge of his nose and groaned. Rachel was the last person he wanted to speak to right now. But ignoring her call would mean having to deal with her wrath later.

He lifted the phone to his ear. "What do you want, Rachel?"

"I want you to drop this custody hearing."

Peter glanced at the calendar on the wall. "You're due to arrive in the states in less than two weeks and you want me to drop it?" He let out a derisive laugh. "I'm not going to do a dang thing. This is happening and if Kat gets taken away from you—"

"You're a hypocrite."

He stumbled over his words then laughed again. "What?"

"You heard me. If you make me come stateside, I'm going to stand before that judge and tell him you went against our agreement."

Shaking his head did nothing to clear the fog. He hadn't done anything to break their arrangement. She'd been the one to force him to take Kat when their daughter was scheduled to be with her mother. "What agreement is that? Because from where I'm standing, you're the one who chose not to be a parent to our child."

"Seriously? That's rich. Either you were deceptive on purpose, or she's been doing stuff under your nose and you're not fit to be a parent."

Peter had to focus on not losing his cool. For all he knew she was egging him on, trying to get him to say something that could be used against him. "How about you enlighten me. What have I been doing that is so terrible?"

She laughed. "So you really don't know? Oh, this just gets better and better. I'd wager you're going to regret putting the stipulation in our agreement that Kat isn't allowed to have a phone until she's twelve and she's not allowed social media accounts without both of us having the password."

A cold chill raced down his spine. She couldn't possibly know Kat had watched videos on someone else's account. Someone else's phone. No different from looking over Tiffany's shoulder. "What are you talking about?" he hedged.

"How about you get on TikTok and look up her favorite little influencer. She's done a stitch with that Quinne Hart she loves so much."

"A stitch?"

"Oh, educated yourself, Peter. She made a type of video which mixes her video with someone else's."

His stomach bottomed out. "She *what*?"

"Exactly. So if I were you, I'd call your lawyer and have this whole thing dropped. Apparently your parenting style should be called two-faced, because you won't allow me to do what you've just been caught doing. Kat has never forgiven me for agreeing to your ridiculous rules and I backed you up."

A lump formed in his throat, so large he couldn't swallow it. They'd had this in the bag. Granted, this new information would only hurt them a little, but it was nothing compared to Rachel's abandonment. He just hadn't wanted to deal with any surprises and this was a big one.

He tuned back in to what his ex was saying. "... I suppose I won't be coming to Atlanta after all."

"Wrong."

"Excuse me?"

"You're still coming. We're taking care of this once and for all. You've taken advantage of my generosity for the last time."

"But the account—"

"If you think for one moment that a social media account is a bigger deal than not showing up, you're sorely mistaken. I didn't authorize any accounts and fully intend to get to the bottom of this one. Thanks for the call, Rachel. I'll see you soon."

"But—"

He hung up the phone and scowled across the room. If the last fifteen minutes had taught him anything, it was that he couldn't trust anyone. He couldn't trust Rachel for obvious reasons. And he couldn't trust Quinne. She'd been the one to set up the account. This was the first time Kat had made a choice to go against his wishes and there was only one difference between the daughter he used to know and the one he had now.

She was spending all of her time with someone new.

His heart crumpled with that realization. If he

wanted to retain any control over this situation, he needed to break things off with Quinne.

Peter was full of nervous energy the longer Quinne was out with Kat. He needed to fix this problem and do it fast to save himself from Rachel's wrath. As soon as he figured out what had happened, then he'd call his lawyer, and...

Dang it!

Did he just add sugar to the soup instead of salt? He spun around and searched the ingredients he'd set out. Okay, good. No sugar.

He was losing his mind over this. The stress of everything was finally getting to him. Peter glanced at the clock on the wall. They should have been back by now. Maybe he should call Quinne.

He should have never have allowed his romantic feelings to come to the surface because when Quinne was just here to help him out with his daughter, she had followed every rule to the letter.

It was only after he'd started getting serious with her that she changed the way she viewed Kat.

His irritation had bloomed into full fury just as his daughter and Quinne entered the kitchen, laughing and chatting as if nothing were wrong. Peter spun toward them, his dark gaze landing on his daughter first. "I need a word with Ms. Hart."

Kat stiffened. She set her wide eyes on Quinne, then swung her focus back to him. "Why do you want to talk to Quinne? Is she in trouble?"

Peter shot a warning look in his daughter's direction. Kat nodded and slunk out of the kitchen. He followed, but only to shut the door. When he turned to face Quinne, her defenses had already gone sky high.

Quinne had her arms folded across her chest. Her expression was guarded but also had notes of irritation. "Ms. Hart? Seriously?"

His eyes narrowed. "Do you know who called me this morning?"

"Obviously not, but it sure put your undies in a bunch."

He could feel the heat rising along the back of his neck, but there was no way to stop it. Peter crossed the floor so he wouldn't be tempted to raise his voice. "My wife called."

"You mean, your *ex*-wife."

Peter scowled. It would have been better to put this conversation on hold until he was calmer, but there was no going back now. "Rachel called to notify me she wanted the custody hearing dropped." When he looked up at Quinne, she appeared mildly shocked but mostly worried.

"Why? Did something happen?"

"You tell me." He snapped.

Her head reared back. "Excuse me?"

He shook his head, the miniscule patience he'd had before now obsolete. "Kat is using that TikTok account of yours. The one you gave her access to. She's making videos and breaking all the rules of my current custody arrangement."

To her credit, Quinne was surprised. "That's not possible—"

"I told you Kat wasn't allowed to have an account. And you went against my wishes."

"I don't understand. She only had use of it on my phone and there's no way she could have gotten onto it without my log in. Which I never gave her."

"Clearly she's figured out a loophole. This could ruin everything, Quinne. I could lose Kat over this."

"I doubt any judge would take this and make it a bigger deal than what Rachel did to you."

"That's just it! There's no telling what a judge might do. What if we get one who agrees with the no-social-media rule? This custody thing could get so much worse. I should have never—" Peter caught himself before he said something he'd truly regret—like saying he should have never asked her out.

She stopped searching on her phone and stared at the screen. Slowly she lifted her eyes and met his gaze. "I'm sorry."

He sighed, the ache in his chest growing. This was not how he wanted things to go. "It's my fault. I should have known better than to believe you'd be ready for this kind of responsibility."

"What?" She spit out sharply.

"You're not a parent, Quinne. You don't understand the weight we have to carry."

Her face flushed a deep crimson color. "Okay, so I make one mistake and suddenly I'm not mother material?"

"That's not what I said."

"Oh, I think I know exactly what you were saying. You don't trust me to spend time with Kat anymore."

"I didn't say that either." Though it wasn't far off from where he was going.

She shoved her phone in her pocket while she shook her head and let out a dark laugh. "It sure feels like it. Until I allowed Kat to use that account you seemed happy with me looking after her. Teaching her stuff and keeping her safe and getting close to her. I'm so confused, Peter because I've seen you hand her your phone to watch YouTube. This is the first I've heard about the rules in the custody arrangement and I might have made a mistake but it wasn't done to hurt Kat. I love her."

"I don't know why *my* rules weren't enough. I shouldn't have to explain myself, Quinne. Kat is my child. You were there to watch out for her."

Quinne's face crumpled. "Is that all I was? Just the hired help who couldn't get it right?"

Peter flinched. Her words stung more than he'd like to admit. His jaw tightened. Having this argument wasn't going to get them anywhere. "This isn't about us. This is about Kat. And she needs a role model who—"

"Who's better than me. Yeah, I get it." Quinne shook her head and walked around the counter toward where she'd set everything up for her videos. "I'll get this stuff out of your hair and make sure I record my videos when you're not working."

A sudden anxiety hit him hard in the chest for reasons he couldn't explain. Breaking up with her was the right thing to do for his family, but he didn't want her to be completely removed from his life. "You don't have to do that."

She stilled, not looking at him. "I don't think it would be a good idea for me to be here when Kat is here —or you. This is going to be for the best." Her eyes continued to avoid his, though her movements became stilted. Finally she headed for the door.

He had no idea what prompted him to step in her path, but he did. She lifted her gaze to meet his.

"Quinne," he rasped. "I'm—"

"Don't. Just... don't." She adjusted the box she carried in her arms. "Goodbye, Peter."

Then she was gone.

Chapter Twenty-One

Every part of Quinne ached. From her head to her chest, it was like all of her organs had gone on strike and refused to do what she needed them to in order to cope. Her last conversation with Peter had been the most difficult one she could remember in her life. It had taken every ounce of self-control to show him she was perfectly fine with their breakup.

But it was more than simply losing someone she had fallen for. She'd lost so much more than that.

She'd lost Kat. She'd lost the newfound feeling of family. She'd lost all confidence that she would one day make a good mother because in a matter of weeks she'd come to realize how much that was something she wanted one day.

If she couldn't even be the kind of role model that Kat needed, then would she ever be able to handle being the parent she dreamed of becoming?

With one statement, Peter had shattered everything she'd wanted for her future.

Quinne sat slumped in the chair seated at a table

with her mother, her mother's friends, and their daughters. Up until this past week, she'd been too busy with Peter and Kat and she'd neglected her visits with them, so it made sense that the second she returned, they'd try to give her all the advice she didn't need.

"You need to stop moping and get back out there," Izzie said. "Just because one relationship didn't work out doesn't mean they *all* won't."

Quinne rolled her eyes, not bothering to give Izzie a retort. Margaret's daughter had married a man whose uncle resided here after being an early victim... recipient, of the matchmaking that went on.

Lucky for Izzie, she'd gotten one of the good ones. Bart was one of those guys who was genuinely good—like Peter—and he adored Izzie so much he'd do anything for her.

Throat closing up, Quinne pulled out her phone, choosing to bury herself in notifications rather than have to deal with this conversation.

"Don't push her, Izzie. Heartbreak of any kind is difficult to overcome." Millie offered a reassuring smile in Quinne's direction. "Don't worry, dear. Things have a way of working themselves out."

Alice nodded to agree with her friend. "Nothing can keep my daughter down for long. You'll bounce back, Quinne, and Peter will realize just what he is missing."

Quinne groaned, sinking farther into her seat. "Do we really have to talk about this? It's bad enough that all of you know him, do you guys have to give me relationship advice too?"

The only one who'd been quiet this whole time was Olivia and Quinne had a feeling it had to do more with the fact that she was marrying the man who bankrolled

Quinne's little project. Maybe she was worried Quinne might abandon the project thanks to the broken relationship.

The conversation around her shifted into something else. With the attention no longer focused on her, she got to her feet and headed out the door that led to the gardens surrounding the main building.

"Quinne, wait up!"

She stiffened then glanced over her shoulder to see Olivia headed in her direction. Great. Perhaps she'd been wrong about Olivia. The woman might have just been holding back her feelings until she was no longer going to be chided by the older women in their group.

"Hey," Olivia murmured as she fell into step beside Quinne. "Where are we going?"

"We?"

Olivia chuckled. "Okay, where were you going before I so rudely hijacked your walk?"

"I dunno. I just needed to get out of there." Quinne took a deep breath of fresh air and released it. Coming to Maple Gardens today had been harder than she'd expected. If she'd had it her way, she wouldn't have stepped foot back in this place at all. But then this was where her only family lived and she couldn't just abandon her mother.

"Yeah, I get it."

Quinne raised a brow. She highly doubted that. She'd seen the relationship Olivia had with Isaac. They were inseparable—that glow of a new relationship still going strong even after all these months.

"It's not what you think," Olivia added. "It's hard having a relationship with someone you work for."

"I don't work for Peter."

Olivia gave her a disbelieving look. “He hired you to help with Kat, didn’t he?”

“Well, yeah...”

“Exactly. That sort of relationship can get messy—especially when you’re dealing with a kid—or so I’ve heard.” She nudged Quinne’s shoulder with her own. “But it’s like they said back there. Things work out. It might not be with Peter, but—”

“It most definitely won’t work out with Peter,” Quinne muttered. She nearly told Olivia exactly what Peter had said, but thought better of it. She wasn’t the type to air her dirty laundry, especially when her ex worked with the person she was speaking with.

“Why not?”

“We... just don’t... fit together. I guess we want different things.” That was the closest she could come to confessing how things had ended between them.

“I don’t buy it. I saw you two together. There’s definitely something there.”

“Yeah? Well, I don’t know what to tell you. I’m just not mother material.”

Olivia’s hand snatched Quinne’s forearm. “Is that what he said?”

Quinne could hear the sharpness in Olivia’s voice, and she immediately regretted letting her own emotions go rogue. “No. Not really. I’m just not ready to be in that stage of my life. I have a lot to learn.”

“Do you think Peter is the perfect parent?” Olivia snorted as she shook her head. “Did he ever tell you he had us all searching the place top to bottom one morning because he couldn’t find Kat? First week he had her visiting.” She nodded at Quinne’s look of surprise. “Yep. And there are other stories like that. Kids are hard. Being a parent is hard. They're all just doing the best they can. So, if you broke up with him because—"

"It doesn't matter why we broke up. It's done. We're over. And I just don't want to talk about it. My life has never revolved around the people I interact with in my daily life."

Olivia frowned. "That's a little sad, isn't it?"

"No, it's not."

"Sure it is. The people in our lives are what make it worth living. We need that connection."

Quinne pulled away from Olivia. "Some connections just don't work out. I'm sorry. I have to go." She tore off down one of the paths that led into the gardens.

The problem with people like Olivia was that they didn't understand what it was like to be an influencer. Sometimes the people in real life weren't as genuine as the people she met online. It wasn't sad. It was just different.

Even as she repeated these things to herself as she slowed her march to a wandering kind of pace, she wasn't so sure she was right either.

Thinking back to when she was the happiest, she had to admit it was when she'd spent those few nights at Peter's place. It had been so easy to pretend that they had a future together. It was terrifying and exciting all at once.

But now that possibility was long gone.

The ache in her chest returned so strongly that it got harder to breathe. She clutched at her chest and shut her eyes before shuffling to the side of the path and taking a seat on a bench. A tear slipped down her cheek, but she brushed it aside and focused on her breathing.

She didn't need anyone.

Not Peter.

Not even Kat.

Just herself and her mother.

The morning the first episode in her new series was released, Quinne couldn't bear to have her phone or any other device on.

It was strange, not wanting to be available to interact with her fans online. Normally, she'd comment on their comments or drop links to the products she used, but today she didn't feel like being put in the spotlight. It was almost like it all felt incredibly wrong. Her career had been the thing that once gave her the most joy, and now it was the thing that did the exact opposite.

There was nothing of value in her videos. The people who knew her didn't really *know* who she was or what she liked. They were all just people who pretended to be her friends. Well, other than Artie, but they both led lives which rarely intersected these days.

Even the in-person events that were held for influencers like her weren't all that great.

It had taken getting to know Peter and Kat to make Quinne realize just what she was missing.

Quinne groaned as she climbed out of her bed and headed into her kitchen. She needed a distraction, but there was nothing she could think of that would be enough to keep her mind off Peter and Kat.

Her social media channel only made things worse. She couldn't go to Maple Gardens. Even being in her kitchen made her think of Peter.

She pulled out a coffee mug and fixed herself a cup of her favorite brew then headed out to the balcony that overlooked a nearby park. She stared out at the people wandering past and tried to come up with stories for each of them. A couple holding hands had just met and he was going to propose soon.

A painful twinge attacked her heart. At one time she'd thought Peter might do the same for her. The fantasy of starting a family had never even been a passing idea until she'd fallen for Peter. He was the one person who made her want more out of life.

And she'd managed to ruin any possibility of that happening.

Kat would always come first for Peter, and she couldn't even be mad at him for ensuring that was what would happen.

It was what made him a good man.

He was a protective father first and foremost.

She should have known better than to think she could just insert herself into his life and everything would be wonderful. Quinne wasn't cut out to be the kind of woman Peter needed and the pain she felt wasn't worth dwelling on.

They hadn't even been dating all that long. She should be able to bounce back, but her impatience seemed to be impeding that ability. It would just take a little more time.

Chapter Twenty-Two

Something was burning.

Peter muttered a curse and jumped up from the couch where he sat watching a movie with Kat. She twisted around to watch him dart into the kitchen and yank open the oven. Smoke billowed out of the appliance and he let out a cough as he waved it away.

So much for fresh oatmeal and chocolate chip cookies.

Peter shot an embarrassed look at his daughter, who gave him a flat look. "Why do you keep burning stuff, Dad?"

He could give her a thousand excuses.

There was the stress of the upcoming custody hearing. The frustration over losing Quinne. And the fact that he had started dreading going to work. He didn't know what days Quinne would drop in to see her mother and it wasn't like he could ask her to leave. She had every right to be there.

His life had turned into a complete mess and he had no one to blame but himself. He should have just left

Quinne alone. Had he been able to control his feelings, none of this would be happening.

As much as he wanted to blame her for everything, he could only blame one person and it was the guy who had lost his multi-year streak of not burning food in his kitchen.

Peter grabbed the pan from the oven and placed it in the sink. The residual water from when he'd done dishes caused the pan to sizzle angrily. He tossed the hot pads on the counter and shut the oven with his foot.

"I guess I was just having too much fun with my favorite daughter." His answer wasn't what she wanted, made clear by the way she rolled her eyes and faced the television. He headed toward the couch, returning to his seat. "Sorry about the cookies. Do you want ice cream instead?"

Kat shook her head.

"How about some popcorn?"

"I'm not hungry." She snuggled up against the arm rest, pulling the blanket that was on her lap up to her chin. "I just miss Quinne."

He'd expected this conversation would come, but even still, he wasn't prepared for it. What was he supposed to say? That he missed her too? Quinne had been more than his girlfriend. She'd been Kat's nanny, tutor, friend, and person she looked up to. Perhaps that was part of the bigger issue at hand. Kat shouldn't have been spending so much time with Quinne. They'd both learned that the hard way.

The movie continued to play, but he'd long since stopped paying attention. The cartoon characters on the screen wouldn't have been able to hold his interest, even if he had wanted to see the movie. Thoughts of Quinne were the only thing to consume his mind since she left. It was funny how, before they'd met, he'd been perfectly content in his life. There were so many things that made him happy—that made his life fulfilling. He had his daughter, his job, this beautiful home... but now all he wanted was to have her back.

Why did he have to go and fall for someone who endangered the most important part of his life? This probably wouldn't have even happened if Kat hadn't been home the last few months. Granted, he wouldn't have gotten to know Quinne nearly as well either.

Peter turned and kissed the top of Kat's head. She lifted her face toward him, and something about the way she looked at him caught him off guard. He pulled away, brows furrowing. "What's the matter?"

Kat looked away, definite guilt skipping across her features. "I don't want you to be mad."

He stiffened. This didn't sound good at all. Did it have something to do with the social media account? Peter couldn't jump to conclusions right now. He had enough on his plate to deal with.

Taking a deep breath, he faced her so they were both sitting cross-legged on the couch. "What is it?" He grabbed the remote and paused the movie for good measure. She needed to know that he was completely committed to this conversation. No more upheaval in their relationship.

Her eyes didn't meet his and she nibbled on her lower lip furiously. "You shouldn't have broken up with Quinne."

His heart hitched, and he could have sworn part of it crumbled off from the rest of it. "Sweetheart, you don't have to worry about that. Sometimes relationships just don't work out."

Kat shook her head, her face flushing with color. "No. You don't get it." When her gaze lifted to meet his, he was surprised to find her eyes brimming with tears. "I could tell you liked her—a lot. I know you did, so don't even lie about it."

"I wasn't going to."

"And she liked you. So why did you have to break up with her?"

Just like that, the rest of his heart fell. His heart broke for the relationship he'd had with her mother. The one he could have had with Quinne, and the one he had with his daughter. On top of it all, he was realizing just how much Kat had grown attached to Quinne. Why else would she be reacting this way?

Peter pulled Kat close, hugging her tight enough to prevent her from crawling away. "It's going to be okay. Like I said, sometimes people come into our lives and they're just gonna be there for a short amount of time. We have to appreciate it—"

"Shut up!"

He froze. Kat had never spoken to him like that before in her life. The fact that she was doing so now only solidified that he needed to do something more to control the situation. Quinne leaving might hurt right now, but it was definitely for the best.

"You didn't have to break up with her and you know it."

Peter pulled away. "Kat—" he started, but she interrupted him again.

"You *loved* her. You loved her maybe even more than you loved Mom."

"What? Where are you—"

"She made you happy, Dad. You smiled more. You were more fun to be around. I know you don't want to hear that, but you shouldn't just end something because it gets hard."

That was it. The straw that broke the camel's back. "Now, you wait one second, young lady. My relationship with Quinne has a lot of working parts. There's more than just how I feel about her to consider. When two people decide they want to be together, they have to see if they can click not only with those feelings, but everything else. Jobs, home life, other family members... all of it has to be figured out. Quinne was wonderful. And you're right. I cared about her a great deal."

"You loved her."

"Yes," he whispered.

"Then you shouldn't have broken up."

He shook his head. How could he tell her that the biggest reason he had to call it off was because of her? That could devastate her. He had to center himself before he could meet her gaze. Peter took a deep breath then let it out, but the effort did nothing to help. "I had more important things to work through besides starting up a new relationship. Dealing with your mother... and some other issues—"

"You mean the TikTok account."

His lips pressed into a thin line. "Yeah. That."

She slumped back against the couch armrest. "Oh. So, it is my fault."

"No. Of course it isn't."

Kat nodded and wiped at her face as a tear slid down her cheek. "Yeah, it is. Tiffany said it would be okay. She said that no one would find out." Her eyes flitted to meet his. "She said that you hated TikTok and you wouldn't even see it. So we did the stitch when I was using Quinne's phone. The night you brought home Chinese for dinner. In my bedroom."

The blood in his body ran cold.

He had been in the house. He'd told Quinne to leave his daughter using the account until Tiffany left.

Peter settled back on the couch and stared at the television that had gone into screensaver mode. Hollow. That was how this realization felt. He didn't regret the decision he'd made to cut Kat off from Quinne. Even his lawyer said that would be the best route to take until the dust settled on the custody hearing.

But now, a part of him wondered if they could have worked things out differently.

"Dad?"

He glanced over at his daughter, and instead of finding that confident young woman who insisted he was wrong, he found his scared little girl. She still had a long way to go, but at least she was on the right track. "Yeah?"

"Are you going to call Quinne?"

Peter let out another sigh as he got to his feet. "No. I don't think I am."

She scrambled after him. "Why? You love her."

He shrugged, heading to the kitchen. "Sometimes things don't work out. Sometimes there's a good reason and others there isn't."

"But there isn't a good reason this time, Dad. I told you the truth. You can stop being mad at her."

He stopped and she bumped into him. Turning, he

looked down at her and dropped to crouch on the balls of his feet. This put her a few heads over him, but it was better than him towering overhead. "You remember when your mother didn't come get you?"

Kat nodded.

"Well, I'm trying to get our custody arrangement changed. It wasn't okay for her to leave you here without telling you or me. It wasn't fair to either of us."

"You didn't want me here?" Her quiet question tore at him in a way he wasn't expecting.

"Of course I want you here. The problem is that we both deserve consistency. That's why I'm preparing to ask for full custody. That means you'd be staying with me all the time and you could go visit your mom when it works in our schedule."

A plethora of emotions crossed her face. He couldn't tell if she was happy or upset by this notion. He prayed it was the former. Peter didn't know what he would do if she told him she didn't want any of this.

Finally her gaze locked with his and she nodded. "I think that's a good idea."

Relief washed over him and he pulled her into a tight hug as his knees fell to the ground. But just as quickly as their hug started, she pulled away.

"I still don't understand why you can't call Quinne and fix things."

Kat was still too fragile for him to tell her that the social media account was the biggest deciding factor. It wasn't just the post that had caused havoc. It was the unsupervised use of the account, too. The custody agreement might have been a little overkill, but at the time they'd both agreed to it. There was no predicting what was going to happen as Kat got older. It would be best to keep her in the dark so she didn't end up blaming herself more than she already had.

"Maybe one day we'll see if we can work things out." It was a cop-out response and he knew it. But it was enough to get Kat to accept where they had finally ended up.

Only, now he didn't know if he wanted to accept it.

Chapter Twenty-Three

For too long Quinne told herself that everything would just work out. Secretly she had hoped that Peter would cool off and that either he or Kat might reach out to her. But it didn't happen.

As much as Quinne wanted to blame Peter for all of the feelings that assailed her on a daily basis, she couldn't. He'd had every right to do what he'd done.

It had been only a few days since her videos had gone out. She'd avoided logging on, but maybe it was time to do just that.

Quinne moved from where she stared out her apartment window toward her desk and opened up her phone. She got into her TikTok account and was immediately inundated with notifications.

More followers.

Comments.

Thousands of shares.

The videos she'd done with the residents had gone viral. From the looks of it, they weren't necessarily popular because of the food or the recipes. The nostalgia over spending time with grandparents had pushed her following to double its size.

Quinne's eyes rounded as she took in what had occurred on this account, before she switched to her other social media platforms.

The same thing was happening everywhere else.

She sat back in her seat, her hand to her head, not sure what she should do. She'd always been popular, but this was insane. Not only did she have the younger demographic, it appeared she'd snagged the older one as well.

Her phone buzzed and she jumped. The caller ID didn't look familiar, but that was a usual occurrence when she was dealing with sponsors or other people her agent sent her way.

"Hello?"

"Have you seen the news?" Isaac's voice burst through the speaker.

Her heart leaped in her chest and she glanced toward the television. "No. Should I have?"

"You probably want to turn it on."

Quinne picked up her remote and aimed it at the television. "Am I looking for any channel in particular?"

"Just a local news station."

She opened her cable guide and found one of the local news stations.

"Her name is Quinne Hart and she's definitely won the hearts of the people in Georgia." A video from her TikTok populated the screen—the one where she was making some baked goodies with Isaac's mother, Millie. They were laughing as they discussed the tips and tricks to the treat. When the clip ended, the newscaster's face returned to the screen.

"Quinne Hart is a local influencer known for her videos on..."

She turned down the volume and settled onto her couch as her legs grew weaker by the second. It was one thing to have her videos go viral. She'd had a few of them do so over the years. But to be on television was something else entirely.

"Okay," she murmured. "It doesn't sound like you're upset."

"Upset? Of course not! Do you know how many calls I've gotten about this? People love you. They love the residents of Maple Gardens. I have companies wanting to coordinate donation efforts to get more of these places opened up and to be made more affordable."

Chills raced down her spine. "That's... amazing."

"I know! And it's all because of you."

She shook her head, her eyes flicking up to the muted television screen as another one of her videos, this one with a resident named Lily, was being showcased. "I didn't do anything."

"Are you crazy? We couldn't have asked for better press. This is going to be the thing that pushes Maple Gardens into the next decade. I don't know if you've noticed, but people don't spend time with their grandparents like they used to. Whenever someone says *retirement facility* or *nursing home*, it has a terrible connotation. What you've done is remind people what it's like to have that warmth back—to have family back. You did that, Quinne."

It felt like she was having an out-of-body experience. Her soul had exited and it was now floating overhead staring down at her. But then she crashed back to ground. It didn't really matter anymore. Along with losing Peter and Kat she'd lost the drive to continue pushing the boundaries on her social media.

"Thank you," she mumbled.

"Thank you? That's all you have to say? For goodness sake, Quinne. Be excited about this! You've turned our world on its side."

"I guess so."

"I have a proposition for you. I don't want to discuss this over the phone, so let's set up an appointment with my secretary. When do you think you could come in?"

A spark of interest poked through the fog of uncertainty. A proposition? That sounded like something that could pull her out of this storm cloud she'd found herself in.

"Quinne, are you still there?"

"I'm here."

"I'll just put you through to my secretary. I look forward to meeting with you, Quinne. Good work." The line clicked and Isaac's secretary came onto the phone.

"Ms. Hart? I have some openings today and tomorrow if you have time to come into the office."

"Sure, I can come in today." It wasn't like she had anything better to do.

"How does two o'clock sound?"

"I can make that work." She'd stop in at Maple Gardens and see her mother for lunch before going. Hopefully she'd be able to avoid Peter altogether.

Quinne stepped over the threshold into the dining area and her eyes immediately found her mother, surrounded not only by her usual friends, but several others. Someone she didn't recognize noticed her. Eyes growing wide, she waved Quinne over excitedly.

"She's here. She's here."

The group separated and her mother got to her feet. "Quinne. Have you heard?"

Quinne's focus swept through the group with surprise.

"We were on the news! On *national* television," Alice gushed. "We're like movie stars."

Alice's enthusiasm touched Quinne. "Yeah, I guess you are."

The women practically pulled her into their little group and pushed her to take a seat. They chattered excitedly, their voices becoming a cacophony of sound.

Funny how simply being surrounded by these women had a way of making everything feel better.

At one point she glanced up from one of the ladies who'd been speaking, and her eyes snagged on Peter.

Blood drained from her face, running cold through her entire body. He had a tray in his hands and his eyes were locked on her. Oh, how she wished she could read his guarded expression. The way he was staring at her made her itch, and she squirmed in her seat.

"What's next?" Someone nudged her and she jumped, finding the woman who was speaking was Lily. She offered a small smile, but her brown eyes sparkled with excitement. "Will you be doing more videos?"

Quinne dragged her attention back to Peter, unsurprised when she found he'd disappeared. She brought her gaze back to Lily. Lifting a shoulder, she let her gaze sweep through the rest of the group. "I'm not sure. Mr. Spencer wants to have a meeting with me after lunch. I guess he has some ideas."

Millie beamed. "I'm sure he has plenty."

Quinne stepped out of the elevator and quietly made her way toward Isaac's office. She'd come here not so long ago to ask permission to use his facility for her videos. Neither one of them had known just how much those videos would take off, but as far as she was concerned, they had both benefited.

Only now, she didn't know what she should do moving forward. Hopefully, Isaac would give her the boost she needed.

Isaac's secretary smiled widely at her when Quinne arrived at her desk. "Mr. Spencer is ready for you. Head on in."

Quinne glanced over to his office door and then back to the secretary. She nodded encouragingly. Well, here went nothing.

Isaac's head lifted the second she opened the door. Then his face broke into the biggest smile she'd ever seen him wear. "There you are. How are you feeling?"

"Well, besides getting messages and calls all day, I guess I'm doing okay."

He nodded. "Yeah, I figured people would start reaching out to you too. How many interviews do you have?"

She shook her head with a wry chuckle. "I'm not

doing any interviews at this time. I'd rather let the dust settle."

Isaac frowned but it was brief. "As they say, bad press is still good press. So good press is even better. The more you get out there and ride this wave, the better it will be for everyone associated with Maple Gardens. You have a real opportunity to help this program grow."

Quinne hadn't moved since she'd shut the door. Still hovering by it, she shifted her weight, hoping she didn't look as nervous as she felt inside. "I suppose you're right. Is that what you wanted to ask me? You want me to do some interviews with you?"

He paused, as if considering what she was saying, then waved his hand dismissively through the air. "We'll table that idea for now. What I called you here for is to hire you."

She nearly choked on her words. "*Hire* me?"

"Yes. I want to pay you a retainer to do content for us. I'd like you to set up some social media accounts for Maple Gardens and put up videos regularly. I'd like the world to see the potential Maple Gardens has—especially as we're in the process of expanding to other states."

"You want me to be your... what? Like a public relations agent or something?"

He shook his head. "We already have one of those. You would be like a media coordinator. Or something like that. Utilize your talents online. This wouldn't just be for followers or to become monetized. This is for the residents at every Maple Gardens to feel like they have a family again."

Her brows furrowed. "What do you mean?"

His happy expression faltered, and he gestured toward the chair in front of his desk. “Are you aware that nearly sixty percent of our elderly residents have no visitors? More than half. When you put our videos online, you stirred the pot. You got people to start caring again. Fifty percent of this demographic have no close relatives. But right now, those fifty percent have a better chance at getting a visitor or a pen pal and it’s all because of you. Something about your videos has touched the lives of the people here—and all over the country. I don’t want to capitalize on it from a business perspective. But I don’t want to see that interest drop, either. I want you to keep doing what you’ve been doing and help me create a family for those without one.”

Once again, her body was attacked by chills. The shiver that rippled down her spine was almost painful. This was the exact kind of thing she’d needed to get her out of this funk.

Quinne nodded. “I’ll do it.

He smiled far too quickly. It was as if he had already known what she was going to say. Isaac nodded. “Great. We’ll set up a few more meetings this week, so we can get everything prepared for launch.” He walked around the desk and held out his hand. “I’m looking forward to working with you.”

She shook the hand he offered. “Me, too.”

Chapter Twenty-Four

The day for the hearing arrived and Kat was in a darker mood than usual. Though she'd confessed to the wrongdoing that had resulted in his breaking up with Quinne, she refused to accept that Quinne would be out of the picture indefinitely.

If he were honest with himself, he'd admit he was refusing to accept the same thing.

Peter stood in front of a mirror, straightening a tie that made him feel like he was being strangled. As much as he had prepared for today, he was most definitely not ready for it. There was no telling what the judge would decide in this case.

Yes, he thought it was cut and dried, but the more research he did on the subject, the more he realized that it was very rare that a judge awarded a father full custody unless the mother was seen as unfit. Rachel was a lot of things, but she wasn't that. She'd made sure Kat was in the care of her father before she'd gone to have some fun. That didn't fit the parameters most judges used when making this decision.

Peter exited his room and headed into the living room, finding Kat sulking on the couch. Her arms were crossed, doing more than enough to show him that she wasn't interested in talking. That was fine. He didn't need to have a conversation with her right now. He needed to go over everything he was going to say to the judge if he had a prayer of winning this case.

Kat's eyes lifted to meet his and she heaved an exaggerated sigh.

"I know you're not thrilled about this hearing today—"

"I don't care about the stupid hearing. You can win or Mom can win, and nothing really changes."

Understanding flooded his senses. Peter rolled his eyes as he shrugged into his suit coat. "If this is about Quinne—"

Kat's hands slammed down into the cushions on either side of her. "Of course it's about Quinne. You're being stupid."

He lifted his brows. "Do you want to try that again?"

Her scowl deepened. "No. Because it's true. You love her and she loves you. You can't just let her get away."

Peter shook his head. "I don't think I can change anything."

"Why not?"

"You'll understand when you're older."

"I'll understand now." She shot to her feet, her face flushing. "I'm not a kid anymore, Dad."

He froze, his eyes taking in his daughter as he attempted to bite back the laughter that threatened to escape. "You most certainly are still a kid."

"No, I'm not. Statistically speaking, kids who go

through hardship are more likely to mature faster than those who don't."

His mouth fell open. That was unexpected. Shaking off his surprise, he moved closer to his daughter. "And what hardship have you been through exactly?"

"You and Mom got a divorce. I move around all the time. It's hard for me to make friends when everyone I do meet ends up forgetting all about me when I'm gone."

Again, her words threw him off. Was it possible he'd been so blinded by his own struggles with being a single father that he had failed to see how it was affecting his daughter? Kat had seemed to be handling things so well. The more he thought about it, the more he realized something. When she'd first arrived, she'd demonstrated just how frustrated she was over being stateside. The longer she stayed the more she opened up. The constant moving had been more than detrimental.

He pulled Kat into a hug. "I'm sorry," he mumbled. "You're right. You've been through more than most kids your age." She mumbled something into his shoulder and he pulled back. "What?"

"Does that mean you'll tell me why you won't give Quinne another chance?"

He contemplated what giving her that answer might mean. She might be more mature than the kids her age, but that didn't mean she wouldn't blame herself if he told her the real reason he needed to keep Quinne out of his life.

Peter worked his jaw then took a deep breath and released it. "I think if we keep our family just the two of us, the judge will be more likely to let you stay with me full time."

Kat scrunched up her face into one of those adorable looks of confusion. "Why would that matter?"

"Because when you broke the rules, you were under her care."

"That's so stupid!"

He gave her a pointed look and her anger dissolved into something more contrite. "Well, it is. I can make my own decisions. What if I had been with Mom instead?"

Peter shrugged. "There's no telling what would have happened in different situations. This is just one of the reasons why I think it's best if we keep Quinne away for a little while."

"A little while? Does that mean you'll try again?"

He pulled her in close for another hug. "I don't know."

The courtroom was full of families waiting to have their case heard.

Peter draped his arm around Kat's shoulder. They'd just been called up and the judge was going over their case. His lawyer sat on his other side and Rachel was across the aisle with her own representation. Peter had to have faith this would work out for the best. It just had to.

Judge Harrison lifted her eyes to Peter's lawyer. "Let's get started, shall we?"

Peter's lawyer stood and started his speech. He cited everything from Rachel's negligence over the years leading up to this particular situation. "It's not the first time Mrs. Edmonds has left Katherine in Peter's custody at times when it was her time to have her. A child needs routine. They need to be able to count on their parents to fulfill their obligations as written in the original agreement." He continued until he touched on every topic they both felt was pertinent to bring up.

Then it was Rachel's lawyer's turn. Besides raising the social media issue, she gave other reasons for the arrangement to remain the same—mostly that Peter worked too much and was relying on hired help to look after their daughter.

Peter huffed, itching to tell the judge about the conversation he'd had with his daughter only hours before. His lawyer placed a hand on his forearm, a reminder to keep calm.

Judge Harrison set her eyes on Kat and Peter stiffened. They'd discussed that he might take the stand and plead his case on his own. But they'd never talked about Kat. The more he thought about it, the more he worried that if his daughter were to take the stand, she'd unravel all the work he'd done.

Peter reached for Kat's hand and squeezed it, praying she'd take that as a hint to not say a single thing. They needed to have faith this was going to turn out the way it was meant to.

Before the judge had a chance to say something more, the doors to the courtroom opened and shut. Hurried footsteps walked down the aisle and someone settled on the bench behind him. The judge's eyes locked onto whomever it was, then her brows lifted.

"Will there be any additional statements?"

"Yes, your honor. My name is Quinne Hart and I'm here to support Mr. Edmonds, and I would love to speak about him as a parent."

Kat gasped and spun around. Peter could feel the heat of Quinne's eyes on the back of his head, and it took everything in his power not to turn around and meet her gaze.

Peter couldn't move. This wasn't good. He hadn't told Quinne about the hearing. He had no idea how she found out about it, unless...

He glanced toward Kat, who offered him a chagrined smile.

Of course.

Rachel stood and slammed a hand down on the table. "Just wait a moment! I—"

Her lawyer tugged at her to take a seat and gave a sharp shake of her head.

Judge Harrison nodded toward Peter's lawyer. "You can have your character witness come to the stand."

Quinne's hand brushed against his shoulder as she passed, sending an army of goose bumps running along his arms. He sucked in sharply, but kept his gaze trained on the judge.

"I only met Peter and Kat a few months ago but knew from the beginning that he is a great father. I saw love and respect from both sides. Peter is firm but fair and would do anything for his daughter. I wouldn't be surprised if he could actually move mountains for her."

Peter shifted his focus to Quinne, his heart hammering. She was staring right at him, her cheeks full of color and her eyes shining with emotion.

"How do you know Mr. Edmonds?"

"I worked for him for a while. Caring for Kat when

he was working…" She forced a smile and took a deep breath. "But I might not have been the best influence—"

"That's not true, your honor." Peter got to his feet, earning a sharp look from both the judge and his lawyer. He cleared his throat. "Ms. Hart helped my daughter come out of her shell. I haven't seen my daughter happier than she was when Quinne was in her life."

"Please don't interrupt, Mr. Edmonds," Judge Harrison responded. "Continue, Ms. Hart."

Quinne met Peter's gaze, brushing at a tear that slid down her cheek. "I made a poor choice when Kat was under my supervision and Peter rightfully terminated the arrangement. That proved to me how seriously Peter takes his responsibility and commitment to Kat. He puts her first and I admire that."

Chapter Twenty-Five

Quinne's hands and legs shook as she climbed down from the stand. She returned to her seat. Peter's comment had flooded her heart with so much joy she wasn't sure what to do with it.

So she sat with her trembling hands in her lap while the rest of the case went forward.

"I'd like to hear from Kat Edmonds, if that is okay with her?," Judge Harrison asked. "Then I will give my ruling."

The lawyer leaned in front of Peter and met Kat's gaze. "Do you want to say anything?"

Kat peeked back at Quinne then warily glanced at Peter. Finally, she nodded firmly. "Yeah. I do."

Peter hadn't looked back to meet Quinne's gaze since she'd sat down. Beyond the small statement he'd made about her, she wasn't even sure he wanted to see her.

Kat sat down beside the judge in the witness box then looked up at the judge. "I love both of my parents."

"I'm sure you do, sweetheart. What we're here to discuss is who you should be living with."

Kat looked from the judge to both of her parents and back again. "If I got to choose, I'd say that I should live with my dad. But I want to see my mom, too. I don't think she shouldn't be able to see me at all. She should still get to have holidays and summer vacations. But maybe not during the school year." Kat met Quinne's eyes and forced a smile. "This year I got to learn a lot. Quinne helped me with my schoolwork and she helped me with my friends. I learned other stuff too. I got to bake and work in the kitchen with my dad. I won't get to do that kind of stuff if I go to live with my mom."

She pressed her lips together firmly and turned to her mother. "I love you, Mom. But I think it's better if I stay with Dad for now." Kat looked down, her eyes locking on something in her lap.

"Thank you, Ms. Edmonds. You may return to your seat."

Kat glanced up at the judge then nodded. "Okay," she mumbled.

All eyes turned to the judge as she shuffled the papers in her hands. "Based on this information, I have made my decision."

Quinne fidgeted in the hallway of the courthouse, wringing her hands as she paced back and forth. Coming was a bad idea. She couldn't believe the judge hadn't awarded Peter full custody. He was clearly the better parent out of the two. It wasn't fair.

She had no idea how he would react when he came out of the courtroom. Quinne probably should leave right now. Peter probably didn't even want to look at her.

The doors opened and it was too late. Peter emerged with Kat at his side, followed shortly by his ex-wife. At least Rachel didn't seem pleased either.

Peter's gaze landed on Quinne and she froze. She didn't have anywhere to escape to. Fire flared to life beneath her skin, causing her face to feel tight and stretched thin. She looked away as Peter had a quiet conversation with his ex and Kat. Then Rachel left with her lawyer and Peter's lawyer did the same.

Suddenly two arms wrapped around her tight. "Quinne! You came. I didn't think you would make it."

Quinne stared down into the happy face of the little girl she'd probably do anything for. This was the girl who, merely by being in Quinne's life, had taught her how to look beyond herself and think about others. She gave Kat a tight hug. "I'm glad I got to see you again."

She felt Peter's eyes on her before she lifted her gaze to see him standing a few yards away. Her stomach flipped over on itself. Quinne swallowed hard and offered a smile she was sure would crumble at the first sign of his irritation. "Hey," she murmured.

"Quinne—"

"I know. I should have told you I was coming. I shouldn't have blindsided you like this, but I just felt like I needed to be here to support you—and Kat. I'm so sorry—"

"*Quinne,*" Peter started again.

She snapped her mouth shut and peered at him, unsure if she was going to burst into tears or not.

Seeing him again was harder than she had expected. To be this close and not be able to run into his arms made her heart feel like it was ripping in two.

"I'm sorry you didn't get full custody," she murmured.

Peter glanced down at Kat then pulled his wallet from his back pocket. He retrieved a bill and handed it to his daughter. "How about you go get something from the vending machine over there while I talk to Quinne."

Kat frowned. Her eyes darted from Peter to Quinne and back. "But—"

Quinne crouched down slightly. "You know what? I'm hungry. If I give you some money, could you pick me out something good?"

Almost immediately, Kat's countenance changed. She nodded and Quinne handed her a few bills from her purse.

"Now, it's very important you get the perfect combination of salty and sweet. I want both. You think you can do that?"

"Yep." Kat hurried away, leaving Quinne alone with Peter—and she suddenly realized it wasn't something she was prepared for. She itched to say something—anything—to fill the silence that had built between them. But the words just wouldn't come. She was a complete coward.

Quinne's gaze dipped to the ground as she waited for what she figured would be a lecture on putting her nose where it didn't belong.

"I'm glad you came."

Her eyes shot up to meet his.

The way he looked at her made her feel naked,

vulnerable beyond any measure she'd experienced since she'd met him. Those eyes drilled into her like a hot knife through butter, melting away any kind of defenses she might have been able to construct.

Peter cleared his throat as he glanced in the direction where Kat had gone. "This is really hard for me..." he murmured, "I've never been all that good at admitting I'm wrong."

Her brows lifted and a shiver shook her to her core.

When his eyes bounced back to meet hers, she knew she was a goner. She was hooked on every last word he uttered. She'd been ensnared and all it had taken was one look and a few words.

He let out a sigh. "But I was—wrong, that is. The way I reacted... it wasn't fair to you or Kat."

"But you're allowed to have rules. Your main job is to take care of your child—" she rambled on, tripping over her words as she went. "I should have seen it—been better—done what you asked—"

'Kat made that stitch when I was there, Quinne. Right under both our noses.' His hand grasped hers, putting an end to her incoherent thoughts. There was a small smile on his face, one that made her insides melt. "I think it's safe to say that we both have our regrets."

She nodded. That was an understatement. "I don't fault you for your decisions. I get it, really, I do. There's so much more at stake when you're a parent. The more I thought about it, the more I realized that there's a reason you needed to protect her from everything that's out there." Quinne flushed and looked away.

She was part of the problem. While her content wasn't bad, it was still something that pulled children away from doing the things she'd enjoyed doing as a kid. Riding her bike down the street with her friends until the lights came on because it was getting dark, trying out for every sport and activity she could convince her mother to let her participate in, and building tree forts with the neighbors were just a few of those things. When she looked up once more to meet Peter's gaze, she found him staring at her with a contemplative expression.

"You're something else, Quinne Hart, you know that?"

"Thank you?"

His hand squeezed hers and he shifted closer to her. "It's a good thing. I haven't met many people who are so willing to consider another person's point of view. I know I struggle with it." He grew quiet for a few minutes and once again the tension grew between them like a cloud overhead. Where were they going to go from here? If he had asked her what she wanted, she would have requested a second chance. She hadn't been able to get him or his daughter out of her head since they had broken up.

But that wasn't up to her.

Still, the way his hand held hers, it made her almost believe they had another chance. Was he offering her the possibility of a future?

"Do you think we could start over?" he whispered, answering the one question that had been plaguing her mind.

"Start over?"

He took her other hand in his. "There will be some stuff to work out with the lawyers, but I don't see why anyone would have a problem with it."

"What about Rachel?"

He made a face. "Rachel isn't going to be thrilled one way or the other. Not only did she lose majority custody, but she lost a lot of the child support she was getting. Since she only gets to have Kat for a few weeks out of the year, a lot will have to change about her lifestyle." Peter squeezed her hand again. "You don't know how much it means to me that you came. I was an idiot for letting you go."

"Yeah, you were."

They both jumped and looked down at Kat who'd returned with an armful of snacks.

Her eyes bounced from one adult to the other. "Quinne made you happy. You don't just let something like that go."

Peter chuckled, swinging his eyes to Quinne. "No, you don't."

Quinne warmed from the inside out. Besides her mother, these were the two people who she could see herself calling her family. They knew her better than anyone and they made her realize there were more important things than a social media channel, fame, and fortune.

Family.

That was the most important thing.

"What do you say?" Peter inched ever closer. "Give me another chance?"

Before Quinne had a chance to respond, Kat butted in. "Of course she's gonna give you another chance, Dad. She didn't come all the way here to say no."

Quinne laughed. "I guess that settles it." She tugged her hands from his and slipped them around his neck. "You're officially stuck with me."

Epilogue

Six months later

Family day at Maple Gardens was always a busy one. There were more mouths to feed and Peter never knew how much food he needed to prepare. Usually he fell short, even when he overestimated what he needed.

This year was even worse. Quinne's shift into the social media PR position had caused a ripple effect. Isaac had implemented an adopt-a-senior program after Quinne's series took off.

More and more people came to be part of the Maple Garden's community, even if they didn't have a relative here.

Peter wiped at his brow as he finished preparing a dish that would soon go out to the masses. The only downside to family day was the fact that he couldn't spend it with the ones he wanted to the most. Kat and Quinne were both out in the fray, spending time with Quinne's mother.

They had all gotten much closer after the court hearing.

Hopefully they would continue to get closer... especially after what he had planned for today.

Peter pulled the small engagement ring from his pocket and examined it, his heart thundering with the thought of asking Quinne to spend the rest of her life with him. It had only been six months, but he knew without a doubt that Quinne was meant to be part of his life—part of the life he shared with his daughter.

Their small family just made sense.

The door opened and he jumped, quickly shoving the ring into his pocket before spinning around to find Quinne entering the kitchen with someone he vaguely recognized. Peter's brows furrowed as he attempted to place the man. He had dark hair and dark eyes. Why did he look so familiar?

Quinne gestured toward the man. "This is Max. He's Lily's son. We were just talking about how wonderful the food was and he said he wanted to give his compliments to the chef."

Peter glanced toward Max, understanding flooding his mind. He'd only seen Max a handful of times. In fact, if he wasn't mistaken, Max only came around on family day—a fact that mildly bothered him. He offered a gracious smile and held out his hand. "Nice to meet you, Max."

Max shook his hand firmly. "As I was telling Ms. Hart here, it's not common that a chef in a place like this gets recognition. I wanted to come and see for myself who was behind the food being prepared."

"Thank you."

"Have you ever considered moving away from retirement communities to catering?"

Peter chuckled. "I've done a handful of catered events."

"Have you?" Max lifted a brow as his smile widened. "Well, then, I'd love to hire you for an event I'm planning."

Peter glanced at Quinne. This had to be a joke, right? This wasn't where he'd thought the conversation was headed.

"For the last decade I've hosted an evening that benefits several children's charities across the nation. Each year I pick one to sponsor and I try to find local businesses to highlight to help out the community. I'd love for you to check your availability and send me your rates for such an event." Max pulled out a business card and held it out to Peter. "I'll be auctioning off goods and services as well, if you'd like to contribute something to that event. It's going to be at the end of next month, I hope six weeks is enough time to prepare."

Peter glanced down at the card then returned his gaze to the man. "I think we could work something out."

A broad smile spread across Max's face and he nodded. "Wonderful. It was a pleasure meeting you, Mr. Edmonds. I look forward to hearing from you." Max exited the kitchen and Quinne immediately let out a squeal of delight. "This is going to be so much fun! You'll let me help, won't you?"

He slipped his hand around her waist as he shoved the card into his back pocket. "Of course I will. I couldn't do it without you." He gave her a quick peck on the cheek then gestured toward the trays of food. "Will you help me bring these out?"

Together they took the food out and placed it on the buffet tables. Peter glanced around the full room, noting that Max wasn't anywhere to be seen. The guy must have taken his leave right after their meeting.

Before he could slip back into the kitchen, Quinne grabbed his hand and dragged him over to the group where her mother sat between her best friends.

Millie reached for his hand and squeezed it. "Isaac said you've outdone yourself. And after Max mentioned how much he liked the food, he's worried you're going to get snatched up." She winked. "I hope he's paying you enough."

Peter chuckled. "Tell him I'm happy right where I am."

Alice sat quietly, her eyes bouncing from Peter to Quinne. He couldn't describe the relief he felt at knowing she approved of their relationship. Peter then glanced toward Lily who sat on Alice's other side, more somber than he expected. She'd always been the more reserved of the bunch, and he couldn't help but wonder if it had to do with Max's quick exit.

"Max asked Peter if he'll cater an event next month. Apparently he does a lot of charitable work with children. Isn't that amazing?" Quinne leaned her head against his shoulder and smiled as the group let out a chorus of agreement.

All except Lily, who seemed to be lost in thought.

Millie leaned forward, reaching over Alice as she touched Lily's arm. "You know who needs to find someone? Max."

The clarity returned to Lily's eyes and she glanced around the group. "I don't know if Max is interested in dating. He's never really hit it off with anyone that I can think of. He might just prefer to stay alone."

"Nonsense," Millie dismissed her. "There has to be someone he would get along with. I don't care how grumpy a guy is, he just needs to find that little bit of sunshine."

"Well... there is one person he used to hang out with, but they were just friends."

Millie's eyes widened and that look Peter had seen many times before flooded her features. "Who?"

Lily glanced around the group again. "Her name is Ava. But I don't know if she's still local. Max doesn't talk about her. But they used to be inseparable when they were kids." Her voice softened and trailed off. "It wouldn't matter, even if she was available. Max wouldn't listen to me if I recommended that he look her up."

"But what if I did?"

Everyone turned their attention to Quinne.

Her smile widened further. "Seriously, if you can give me her full name, then maybe we can invite her to the charity auction and see if they rekindle anything."

Peter nearly blurted out this was a very bad idea, but then he thought better of it. Quinne wasn't going to be setting them up. She was just going to put them in the same room. What could go wrong with that? From the looks of it, this little plan of theirs was boosting the morale of the group anyway. As long as he wasn't dragged into their little matchmaking schemes, he was fine with it.

"Speaking of unexpected romance, I have something to ask."

All eyes turned toward him and that was when he realized they'd shifted their conversation already. His statement had nothing to do with their speculation that the barista at the local coffee shop might be the Ava who Lily was talking about.

He cleared his throat and dug into his pocket. "I need to do this before the darned ring burns a hole in my pocket," he muttered more to himself than anyone else and dropped onto one knee.

Quinne gasped and Kat jumped up from her seat but didn't utter a word. Her wide eyes shone with excitement, but it was Quinne's gaze that Peter sought.

Surprisingly, she didn't seem the least bit shocked. Her soft smile and knowing gaze proved she probably knew this was coming. Of course she did. The woman was far more intuitive than anyone he'd met.

The only words he was able to utter were, "Will you —" when she threw her arms around his neck, nearly toppling them both to the floor.

Quinne peppered his face with kisses, followed by a long, breath-stealing one. She pulled back mere inches, her eyes delving into his. "I thought you'd never ask."

"You knew, didn't you?" he whispered, his voice low enough no one could hear it over the cheers of those in their little group.

"Yeah, but what do you expect when you keep pulling it out to admire it."

He chuckled, slipping it onto her ring finger. "In my defense, it *is* a pretty nice ring."

She studied the ring on her finger then smiled at

him. “But not as nice as you.” Her kiss sent his heart into overdrive, making his whole body erupt with heat. Quinne was everything he never knew he needed and everything he'd wanted.

His life was complete.

About the Author

Phillipa lives just outside a beautiful town in country Victoria, Australia. She also lives in the many worlds of her imagination and stockpiles stories beside her laptop.

She writes from the heart about love, dreams, secrets, discovery, the sea, the world as she knows it... or wishes it could be. She loves happy endings, heart-pounding suspense, and characters who stay with you long after the final page.

With a passion for music, the ocean, animals, nature, reading, and writing, she is often found in the vegetable garden pondering a new story.

Free short book when you join Phillipa's monthly newsletter (book chat, pets, gardens, puzzles, first-looks and competitions).

www.phillipaclark.com

Also by Phillipa Nefri Clark

Detective Liz Moorland

Lest We Forgive

Lest Bridges Burn

Lest Tides Turn

Connected to this series through several characters is

Last Known Contact

Rivers End Romantic Women's Fiction

The Stationmaster's Cottage

Jasmine Sea

The Secrets of Palmerston House

The Christmas Key

Taming the Wind

Temple River Romantic Women's Fiction

The Cottage at Whisper Lake

The Bookstore at Rivers End

The House at Angel's Beach

Charlotte Dean Mysteries

Christmas Crime in Kingfisher Falls

Book Club Murder in Kingfisher Falls

Cold Case Murder in Kingfisher Falls

Plan to Murder in Kingfisher Falls

Festive Felony in Kingfisher Falls

Daphne Jones Mysteries

Daph on the Beach

Time of Daph

Till Daph Do Us Part

The Shadow of Daph

Tales of Life and Daph

Bindarra Creek Rural Fiction

A Perfect Danger

Tangled by Tinsel

Maple Gardens Matchmakers

The Heart Match

The Christmas Match

The Menu Match

The Cookie Match

Doctor Grok's Peculiar Shop Short Story Collection

Simple Words for Troubled Times

(Short non-fiction happiness and comfort book)

---

www.ingramcontent.com/pod-product-compliance
Lightning Source LLC
Chambersburg PA
CBHW010302100726
47904CB00011B/2715

9780645786231